Hook

MEN OF INKED: SOUTHSIDE

Chelle Bliss
xoxo

Grmm
Blin
xox x

Hook
Men of Inked: Southside

by
Chelle Bliss

To my crazy, fun Uncle…

*Thank you for always making me laugh and being there
by my side during the good times and the bad.*

I'll love you always, Fabrizio.

Chelle, xoxoxo

HOOK COPYRIGHT

Hook @ Bliss Ink LLC

Published by Bliss Ink & Chelle Bliss
Published on January 15th 2019
Edited by Silently Correcting Your Grammar
Proofread by Julie Deaton & Rosa Sharon
Cover Photo @ Allan Spiers Photography
Cover Model: Sebastian Burka

PROLOGUE

ANGELO

How do you say goodbye to the person you thought you had a lifetime to love?

"I'm so tired," Marissa whispers so softly I barely hear her.

I squeeze her hand gently, trying not to hurt her. "It's okay, baby. Rest." But the last thing I want is for her to close her eyes. Every moment that ticks by is one I can't get back, and I know the end is near.

I never thought I'd be here, sitting beside my wife's bed, speaking our final words a week before her thirtieth birthday.

"I won't leave you." I brush the hair away from her face as she closes her eyes.

The day the doctor said Marissa had stage four cancer, the world came crashing down around us. I knew the horrors. The reality of what would happen. I understood her chances of survival were infinitely small, but still, I hoped she'd defy the odds.

Nothing could've prepared me for the months of treatment or these last few hours I've sat with her, watching her light slowly fade.

My family has been supportive, doting on Marissa and me for months. They wanted us to focus only on fighting the cancer that was growing out of control inside her. They took care of everything else, including the kids.

Jesus.

The kids.

Every time I look at their tiny, innocent faces and realize all the things Marissa will miss, they'll miss, I'm completely and utterly wrecked.

The birthdays. The boo-boos only Mommy can kiss and make better. The first loves and broken hearts. The graduations. The weddings. All the milestones, big and small—Marissa won't be there for any of them. I will have to be father and mother, strength and comfort, guiding my children without her by my side. It terrifies me.

I'm not sure I can do it. Right now, I can barely take care of myself. I'm too busy worrying about her and about the future for the little people we brought into this world, vowing to raise them together. Never for a minute did I think one of us wouldn't be around to see them grow into adults.

I try to hold back the tears, vowing to stay strong for my wife in her final hours as she battles through the pain while she tries to comfort us in our grief. She's always been worried about everyone except herself. While the cancer ravaged her body, she wanted the children to know they were loved and that even when she wasn't there to kiss their soft cheeks, she would be watching over them, loving them from afar.

She's always been selfless. That's the thing that drew me to my wife. Her ability to love and give unconditionally without expecting anything in return. I love her with every ounce of my being and have done everything in my power to be the best husband possible—the one she deserves. But no matter how hard I love her, I can't stop death from taking her away from me...from us.

For months, I've mourned her like she's already gone. That's the bitch about cancer. Mourning isn't saved for after the person dies. The process of grieving starts the moment you hear the diagnosis.

Even if there's a glimmer of hope and you want to believe they'll get better, there's always a part of your heart and mind that knows the final outcome and lives in constant fear.

I've spent months with an ache so deep in my chest, my heart feels like it's broken into a million pieces, scratching at my insides as my soul slowly dies along with my wife.

I know as Marissa's spirit drifts away, my ability to love goes with her. When I said the words "until death do us part," I never expected her to go first, and certainly not so soon. I thought we had decades. A lifetime of memories to build together, children to raise, and love to share with one another. I thought we'd grow old together, dying of weak bodies well into our nineties, but never now.

Never so young.

I haven't left Marissa's hospice room in a week except for a few hours to shower, change clothes, and check on the kids.

The day she stopped getting out of bed was the day I set everything else aside to be with her. I knew the kids needed me, but I had a lifetime to be with them and only days or hours to spend with the greatest love I'd ever known.

"I'll give you two some privacy." My mother places her hand on my shoulder and squeezes.

I almost forgot she was in the room. She's been so quiet and unlike herself.

I lean over the bed, staring down at the bracelet on Marissa's wrist, trying to hide my tears.

"I'll be right outside." Ma stands at my side near the bed.

I lift my gaze to Marissa, wiping away the tears before she can see them. "Thanks, Ma." My voice cracks on the last word.

I can't keep my shit together anymore. For months,

I've been able to remain strong, only letting myself fall apart in private. But now, as the minutes pass too quickly, I'm unable to control the agony from seeping out.

My mother steps in front of me and bends forward, placing her lips against Marissa's forehead much like she did to us when we were children. "My love," Ma whispers softly and closes her eyes, choking back the tears. "Rest now, my sweet girl. I will love you for all eternity."

It's a goodbye.

My mother knows the end is near. I know the moment I've been dreading marches closer, and there's nothing I can do to stop it.

For the first time in my life, everything is out of control. I'm completely powerless.

Tears slide down the sides of Marissa's face as she struggles to whisper, "I love you, Mama."

I close my eyes, sealing them so tightly and wishing I could give my life for hers. I'd do anything to be in that bed in her place, feeling everything she's feeling, giving her another chance at life, and taking away her pain.

My wife deserves as much. That's my job as her husband. I'm supposed to protect her.

I've failed miserably.

I want to go back, redo every moment, every kiss, every day, reveling in the seconds instead of letting them pass as we waste hours in doctors' offices and chemo-therapy trying to save her life.

She fought for me.

Fought for our kids.

Fought for our future.

But no matter what she did or how hard she tried to stop the cancer growing inside her, nothing worked. Not a goddamn thing made any difference. Our biggest fear was realized, leading us to this moment. This place. This devastating end.

We stare at each other in silence as my mother walks out of the room, closing the door behind her. Marissa's so frail lying in the hospice bed after months of treatment. Her bones are practically poking through her skin in some spots. Every inch of her body has been ravaged by cancer and the poison they injected her with, trying to buy her more time, but unable to save her life.

"I don't have much time," Marissa rasps. "You need to listen to me." She squeezes my hand with the little bit of strength she has left.

I can't take the distance between us. Sitting in a chair beside her is too far. I crawl into the bed next to her and lie on my side, careful not to hurt her. She tries to move closer but doesn't have the energy anymore. I pull her against me.

She peers up at me with her head on my bicep and her blue eyes piercing my soul. I can't take my eyes off her. I'm filing away these moments because I'm not sure how many more times I'll hold my wife in my arms.

"There's nothing you need to say. I love you, baby. I love you more than anything in the world," I tell her, somehow stopping myself from choking up.

"Angelo," she whispers, and I wonder if it's the last time I'll hear her say my name. She runs her tongue along her dry, cracked lips, and when I lean back to grab the water near her bed, she stops me. "Let me say this."

I nod but don't speak.

I can't.

"We both know I'm dying," she says like she's accepted her reality even if I haven't.

"Baby." I pull her closer and place one hand on her bony hip and the other against her back, feeling absolutely helpless. "Don't say that."

We've never said those words out loud. Saying them makes it real, and even in this moment, with her gasping for air, I find it hard to believe.

"You need to promise me..." She starts to cough, and I hold my breath, praying she'll hang on just a little longer.

My stomach twists and my chest aches because I know the worst hasn't even yet begun. "Maybe you shouldn't talk, love. It's too much."

The tears that seem to have been in my eyes for months are falling down the sides of my cheeks, but I don't dare let go of my wife to wipe them away.

"Promise me you'll love again," she begs.

"I can't," I whisper.

"Promise me, Angelo. I want our children to have a mother and you to have a wife. I can't leave this world knowing you'll be alone."

I wipe the tears away from her cheeks and cradle her face. "No one can fill your shoes. No one. I can never love another soul the way I love you."

"Promise me," she begs again, breaking my heart into a million little pieces. "I need peace."

"I promise, Marissa."

I'm an asshole for lying to my wife on her deathbed, but how can she possibly think I'll ever love again?

Marissa exhales like the weight of the world has been lifted off her shoulders, and she buries her face in my chest, like she does every night before she falls asleep. I hold her tighter, careful not to hurt her, silently begging for a last-minute miracle.

"I love you," I whisper over and over again, unable to stop myself. I rock her gently in my arms, inhaling the scent and softness of her skin. I'm memorizing every inch of her body, every smell that surrounds her, and soaking it all in for the moments I know I won't be able to.

Her body goes still, and I don't hear her breathing. My heart stops, and I hold my own breath, listening for any sign my wife is still with me.

She lets out a long, shaky exhale.

"Marissa." I release my hold on her back so I can see her beautiful face. "Baby."

Her eyes are glassy. She's barely breathing and not

moving. She's staring in my direction, but it's as if she's looking right through me instead of at me.

"Marissa," I say a little louder than before as panic sets in. She doesn't even blink. "I love you," I tell her again.

I resist the urge to scream, knowing the end is closer than it's ever been before. I take another moment to stare into her beautiful blue eyes, praying she can see me and hoping I'm giving her comfort.

"You're my everything."

I want to tell her not to go, but it's selfish. Her body's shutting down, and she's ready to leave the pain behind, even if I'm not.

I never will be.

I place my lips against her forehead, humming the song that played at our wedding. It's the only thing that keeps me sane as I finally come to grips with the fact that my wife isn't going to get better.

She's leaving me.

Her breathing changes again as her body struggles to live and is fighting an unwinnable battle. There's a rattle deep in her chest as her lungs fill with air, and she barely exhales. Her breathing is violent and scarier than I'd ever imagined.

"Baby, you can go. I promise to always love you and make you proud. I'll watch over our babies and take care of them." I barely manage to get the words out without losing control.

The world's spinning, crashing down around me in the most horrific way.

"I love you," I whisper again because I can't say it enough.

When she takes her last breath, a piece of my heart dies too.

CHAPTER ONE

ANGELO

"You need to go out, Daddy." Tate climbs into my lap, blocking my view of the football game. She places her tiny hands on my cheeks, forcing me to look at her and talk about something I've been dancing around for far too long. "Are you listening to me?"

She's so much like Marissa—so full of life with a side of sass, and her bossiness is off the charts too. If I didn't know better, I'd think she was twice her age. She grew up way too fast because of Marissa's death, and no matter how hard I tried, I couldn't shelter her from the pain.

I glance down and give her my full attention. "I'm listening, baby girl."

She tilts her head like she's about to lay shit out for me. "Brax needs a mommy."

My head jerks back at the straightforwardness of her comment. "He has one," I tell her, sweeping her hair behind her ear, wishing I never had to have this conversation with her.

"She's not here anymore, Daddy. Brax needs one, and so do I."

Her words are like a knife through my heart. I can't speak. I'm too choked up by the truth my little girl is dropping in my lap.

She pushes harder against my cheeks, smooshing my face together until my lips pucker. "Mommy won't be mad, Daddy. She wants you happy. It's time for you to get back out there."

This kid. Where does she come up with this stuff? Even though my eyes are filling with tears, I can't stop myself from laughing.

"Where did you hear that?"

"Auntie Nee. She said you need to get back in the saddle and ride that horse. I don't know what a horse has to do with anything." Tate lifts her tiny palms up near her shoulders and shrugs. "I mean, I don't know where we'd put one, but I've always wanted a pony, Daddy."

Thanks, Daphne.

"Oh, sweetheart." I don't have the heart to tell her Daphne wasn't actually talking about a horse. Sometimes my family forgets that although the children are small, they're soaking up every word they say and filing it away in their heads.

She moves her face closer. "I'm serious, Daddy."

God, how I love these moments with her. I know soon enough she'll grow up and will barely look at me. But right now, she stares at me with those big blue eyes, the same ones Marissa had, tugging on my heart.

"Okay, Tate. I'll see what I can do."

She places her tiny, wet lips on mine as she pulls my face to hers. "You made me happy," she whispers as she peers into my eyes.

There's nothing in the world I want more than for my kids to be happy. They're the reason I'm still breathing and not buried beside my wife.

I don't think I could've survived losing her without my children. I most certainly wouldn't have been able to get out of bed, or else I would've ended up an alcoholic, drowning my sorrow in the bottom of a bottle so I wouldn't have to feel anything anymore.

Tate pulls away with her lips still puckered and covered in spit...hers, not mine. She's the sloppiest kisser ever. I pray to God she stays that way, so the boys don't start pounding down the door in a decade.

"I'm tired." She yawns and is superdramatic about it. She stretches her arms and practically shakes in my lap. "Tuck me in."

"Already? It's early, baby."

She slides down my leg until her sock-covered feet touch the floor. "Come on." She tugs at my arm.

Tate loves her sleep. If I let her, she'd stay in bed half the day. She definitely didn't get that trait from me.

"What jammies are you wearing tonight?" I lift her into my arms and carry her toward her bedroom.

"Unicorns." She caresses my earlobe, something she's done since she was a baby. "No. Mermaids." She pauses. "Maybe rainbows."

This is our nightly routine. She rattles off every nightgown in her collection, unable to make a decision. It doesn't bother me. I want to keep her this age forever, arguing over unicorns and mermaids instead of boys.

"How about your princess nightgown?"

Her face brightens. "Yes. Princesses. That's what I want." She bounces in my arms.

I get her changed quickly, a task I've somehow mastered since Marissa died. Tate doesn't always make it easy, usually wiggling or getting sidetracked by some shiny object in her room.

I toss her tiny dress into the dirty clothes basket as she twirls in a circle. "Climb into bed, and I'll grab a book."

She leaps into bed, sliding across the sheets. "I want the kangaroo book," she tells me, bossy as usual.

Right up until the very moment she closes her eyes, the girl is full of attitude.

I stretch out next to her, grabbing the kangaroo book from the nightstand as she curls into my side. "Close your eyes, baby." I open to the first page and start to read until she pokes me in the chest.

"I love you, Daddy."

"I love you too, bug." I kiss her forehead, wishing I could keep her this small forever.

As soon as she's asleep, I dial Daphne to have a little heart-to-heart with her. My sister means well, but sometimes she needs to remember who her audience is and how her words may affect them.

"What's up, Ang? Missing me?"

"Sister."

"What?"

"We need to have a little talk."

She lets out a very dramatic sigh. "I'm busy being a human buffet over here. All this baby does is eat. I swear, if I ate this much, I'd have an ass bigger than Old Lady Benedetto. What's wrong now?"

"Tate heard you say I need to get back in the saddle."

Daphne snickers, getting a little joy at my expense. "Well, you do."

I groan. "Now she wants a horse."

Daphne's laughter grows louder. "The kid has big dreams. Can't blame her for that, brother. I like her style."

Of course she would.

"Sister, don't fill her head with the impossible."

"A horse?" She pauses. "Or you ever having a girlfriend?"

I rub my temple, trying to massage away the tension that never seems to vanish. Why did I even bother having this conversation with Daphne? I knew what she'd say. We've been talking— Scratch that. She's been on my back about this for months.

"Both." I grit my teeth.

"Marissa's been gone a few years now. You need someone to love. It's time."

It's time? My life isn't an appointment or a recipe cooking in the oven. There're no rules when it comes to mourning and moving on. I don't know why everyone in my family thinks it's time for me to start dating.

I don't.

And I'm pretty fucking sure my opinion is the only one that matters when it comes to my life, my kids, and my heart.

"I have someone," I snap.

"Angelo, I love you, but eventually you're going to have to open your heart again. Marissa wouldn't want you to be alone."

"I know." I hang my head, hearing my wife's voice and the promise I made to her. "I'm just not ready."

"I don't think you'll ever be. Just don't wait too long. I swear I saw a gray hair on your head last week."

"Fuck off with that."

I know she's yanking my chain the way she always does because that's her lot in life. Ballbuster extraordinaire and way too much like my ma.

"Anyway, you messed around with Michelle for far too long. You two never would've worked. It's time for you to find someone to really settle down with."

"What?" I stare at the phone, mouth hanging open, wondering how she knows. "I don't know what you're talking about."

"Oh please, Angelo. I'm not stupid or blind. I know you two have been fooling around for a few months."

"Well…"

I thought Michelle and I were stealthy in our hookups and that my entire family, including my sister, was in the dark.

Clearly, I was wrong.

"She's my best friend, dumbass. You don't think I notice shit?"

"We were never serious, Daphne."

"You've slept with her, right?"

"I don't want to talk about it."

"Michelle left for California a week ago. Your time with her is over. You've practiced the gallop, now it's time to trot."

"What the fuck are you even talking about?"

"Figure it out. I got to go. Get your head out of your ass before the rest of your life passes you by. Sweet dreams," she says and ends the call before I can reply.

I toss the phone on the coffee table and kick back, relaxing into the couch to watch the last quarter of the game. But every throw and run goes by in a blur.

I can't stop thinking about what Daphne said.

I replay the last words Marissa and I spoke to each other and how I promised her I'd find happiness again. The closest thing I've come to that has been with

Michelle, but every time I touched her, I was filled with so much guilt.

We were never meant to be more than a fling. I scratched her back, and she scratched my...well, you know. But her plan was always to move to California to take care of her mother who's been battling early onset Alzheimer's for years.

I'm not heartbroken over her leaving. I like Michelle, hell, I even love her. She's been in my life since we were little kids, and it's hard not to have feelings for the woman. But it's not the deep love I have for Marissa.

I can't seem to let go of the past. The memory of my wife and the love I have for her still burns in my heart as strongly as the day she took her last breath.

CHAPTER TWO

ANGELO

"THERE GOES THE NEIGHBORHOOD." Carlos, a regular at Hook & Hustle, slides onto the barstool. "Did you see the joint next door?" He pitches a thumb toward the window and shakes his head.

Carlos looks like he stepped right out of a halfway house before he wandered in. The man has money, but he refuses to wear fancy clothes, preferring to look like a regular schmuck than a man of means.

I grab a clean glass from under the bar top, already knowing his order without his having to say a word. "It'll be fine."

Every old-timer thinks the neighborhood's going to shit because a new store or some swanky new restaurant is hanging their awning over the door. What they see as a demise of their old life, I think of as progress and the bettering of the community. It's always doom and gloom with this bunch. When they're not complaining about the neighborhood, they're rehashing the olden days, which from what I remember, weren't so fucking great.

Carlos stares at me with a straight face and his arms out wide. "I mean, who da fuck needs an entire store of cupcakes?"

"I miss the days when pimps and prostitutes were on every corner," Wally, a complete drunk and asshole, tells us like it's the most normal thing in the world. "Those were the good ole days. The only Cupcake I want is the one who gives me a five-dollar blow job and doesn't complain."

Wally's about seventy years old and used to have a nice wife and was halfway normal. About ten years ago, she caught him banging the maid, and all hell broke loose. She took his ass for every dime they had and left him with nothing except the clothes on his back and the case of chlamydia the maid gave him as a parting gift.

"Dude," I grimace, grossed out by the very thought of some toothless, drugged-up hooker going down on my cock for five bucks in the alley. "You're fucked up, Wally."

Carlos turns to face Wally, one eye looking at him and the other still on me. "You know Cupcake was a man, right, Wal?"

Usually, I barely notice Carlos's lazy eye, but moments like this make it damn near impossible to ignore. I never know where to freaking look, and he's never told me either. I think he likes to keep it a secret just to fuck with my head, and for that reason alone, I love him.

Wally's head jerks back. "What?"

Carlos laughs and slaps the bar top, almost falling over. "I thought I had bad eyes, but come on, man. Cupcake had a five-o'clock shadow and absolutely no tits."

Wally's face turns a few shades of green, and he covers his mouth. "You're lying," he says from behind his hand.

"What was Cupcake's real name, then?" Carlos raises an eyebrow above the eye that's looking right at Wally.

Wally rubs his chin and is silent for a few seconds. "Terri."

"Point made." Carlos straightens, knowing full well he just ruined his buddy's entire day. "You got a helluva blow job from a dude, my man."

"I'm not gay," Wally blurts out like he needs to justify something, which he doesn't.

"No one said you were, dumbass. But there was a reason Cupcake was the cheapest hooker on the block." Carlos is pretty satisfied with himself and does nothing to hide his glee at Wally's agony.

"Well, fuck," Wally whispers, finally coming to the

realization that his bargain-basement BJ wasn't as amazing a deal as he originally thought.

Johnny strolls through the front door, flanked by two bodyguards. "You see the fucking joint next door?" He ticks his chin toward his men before they shuffle into the booth nearest the door, watching for any trouble.

"How's the arm?" I dip my head toward the sling around his chest and the cast still covering the lower half of his arm. The bullet shattered his radius and ulna into a million little pieces, leaving him pretty fucked up but lucky they didn't have to amputate.

"Still fucked." Johnny shrugs before taking the seat next to Carlos. "But I'm upright and alive."

"Lucky fucker," Wally mutters behind his beer glass.

"They ever catch the hooligans that did that?" Carlos asks Johnny but doesn't look at him.

"Stupid shits picked the wrong guy to carjack. They caught them because I popped one of them in the ass as they tried to run away." Johnny laughs, grabbing the beer from my hands before I have a chance to set it down. "Funniest shit I've ever seen."

I stare at the three of them, all single, all sitting at a bar in the middle of the day with no woman waiting for them at home.

One day, if I'm not careful, it'll be me sitting on that barstool talking shit. I'm sure the kids will visit their old man from time to time, but I'll have nothing to sustain me from day to day.

"Back to the joint next door." Johnny wipes away

the foam clinging to his mustache. "Did you get a good look at the piece of ass working in there?"

Part of me loves these guys, but they're way beyond old-school and so crass when it comes to women that sometimes I have to restrain myself from punching them in the face. If there were other customers here at this time of day, I'd shut their shit down. They know it too. But since the bar is empty, I let them have their say with only the occasional glare.

"She's a sweet little thing." Wally licks his lips like the creep he is.

"You two are sick fucks. She could be your daughter for Christ's sake," Carlos tells them, as if he's not a pervert just like they are, which is laughable.

"I have a son." Johnny smirks. "No hair off my balls."

I throw the dish towel over my shoulder and lean against the bar. "You guys better start being a little more respectful to women. If Daphne were here…"

"Don't tell her." Wally's eyes widen as he waves his hands in front of him. "She'd kick me right in the balls."

"I'd pay money to see that." Carlos laughs.

There's a loud noise like a bomb's gone off nearby. Johnny's men are on their feet, surveying the outside, looking for any imminent threat to his life.

"Street's clear, boss," the thick-necked guy in the black suit says as he stands near the door.

"What the fuck?" Carlos clutches his chest as the color starts to return to his face. "I thought I was dying."

"I almost shit myself." Wally laughs and shakes his head.

"And that's different how?" Carlos teases Wally.

Whatever happened, it can't be anything good. The brick between our two businesses is thick and helps as a sound barrier.

"Stay here." I throw the towel on the bar. "Watch the place for me while I check it out."

"Take Maurice with you," Johnny says over his shoulder before I can make it to the front door.

I stop, turn around, and put my hands up to stop the two lugs from following me. "No. I got this."

The last thing I need is two mafia goons at my side when I knock on the front door of the cupcake shop. The girl would probably have a heart attack if she's still alive inside after whatever the fuck happened.

From outside, I don't see anything out of the ordinary. There's an empty display case, a ladder in the middle of the floor, and other construction material, but the store looks in top shape and just as it did when I came in a few hours ago.

"Hello," I call out as I pull the door open just enough to stick my head inside. "Anyone here?"

There's banging coming from the back. "Fucking shit." I hear the woman screech. "You're a mother-fucker. You almost killed me, you piece of shit."

My eyebrows shoot up as I step inside.

"Hello," I yell a little louder.

Whomever she's yelling at sure is getting their ass

chewed out. I don't know if I should laugh or feel bad for the poor sucker.

Marissa used to yell like that sometimes. Especially when she was pissed at something. She never took her anger out on anybody, but objects…they were fair game.

I stand there, frozen and not sure if I should cut my losses and leave, or make sure everything is okay before I head back to the bar to keep the guys from draining a keg.

Taking a step forward, I brace myself for whatever I'm about to find on the other side of the door.

The last thing I expect is to see a woman standing by herself, covered in baking flour from head to toe, kicking the shit out of her electric mixer.

"Ma'am." I clear my throat.

She spins around, eyes wide and wild. "Fuck," she hisses and clutches her chest. "You scared the shit out of me. You should warn a person before you sneak up on them."

There's a twang to her voice, and it's charming.

"I yelled." I smile, trying to show I'm friendly, which I kind of am. On a good day. "A few times."

She rubs her cheeks with the backs of her hands, smearing the white powder. "Oh." She gives me a pained smile. "Sorry about that."

"Everything okay in here? I heard a loud noise. Thought I'd check to see if everything was okay."

She points to the mixer near her feet. "Besides my

batch of turtle cupcakes being completely ruined, I couldn't be better." She swats at her skirt, kicking up more flour into the air and coughs.

We stare at each other for a minute.

Her eyeing me. Me eyeing her.

"Would you like some help?"

"With the cupcakes?" Her eyebrows rise.

"I'm a shit cook, but I can at least pick up the mixer for you. It looks pretty heavy." I let my gaze travel down her body, landing on her way too high heels for cooking. "I'm sure those shoes weren't built for manual labor."

Fuck. The woman's body is mint. Even covered in flour, I can tell whatever's underneath is nothing short of spectacular. The guys said something about her being a piece of ass—their words, not mine—and I hate to say it, but I don't think they were wrong.

"You'd help me?" She takes a step forward and grabs at her pearl necklace. "You'd help a stranger?"

"Ma'am, I may not know you, but when there's a lady in need, it's my duty to help."

"Say that again," she tells me, piercing me with her moss-green eyes.

"Which part?"

"All of it, handsome. All of it." She smirks.

Fuck me. We have a live one, and from the looks of her, she has every ingredient necessary for an absolute recipe for disaster.

CHAPTER THREE

TILLY

Goodness me.

This tall drink of water standing in front of me is straight out of every grown woman's fantasy. His jeans and black T-shirt hug his body in all the right places, clinging to his skin like there's nowhere else they'd rather be. I get it. If I were that close to his body, I'd hold on for dear life too.

His jawline is nothing short of spectacular—chiseled and covered with enough stubble to feel like sandpaper underneath my fingertips.

"Ma'am?" His voice is a little deeper than before but every bit as sexy. "Are you sure you're all right?"

Be bold.

I hear Roger's words echoing in my head. He's told me more than once it's time for me to step outside my comfort zone and get back to the way I used to be. Easy for him to say. But being a single woman after years of marriage and trying to traverse the world of dating in this decade isn't something I've found easy.

Go after what you want, Tilly. And right now, I want a dose of tall, dark, and handsome.

"My name's Chantilly, like the lace." I can't wipe the dumb smile off my face because everything about him makes my body sing. "But you can call me Tilly or…you know…" I take a step forward and place my hand on the steel table, batting my eyelashes a little. "*Yours* works just fine too."

He looks at me funny, maybe not catching my flirtation or thinking I need a straitjacket and a padded room. Maybe I do. I'm coming on strong, but I've never been shy a day in my life. Though, this is way too much even for me.

"Tilly," he says, preferring that name over the other one, which is fine but not where I was hoping this was headed.

When he drags his hand through his hair, everything clicks. The gold wedding band around his finger glistens in the overhead lighting like a warning beacon for me to keep my distance.

All the good ones are taken or so fucked-up, there's no one who wants them. Maybe he's a little of both. Or at least, that's what I tell myself to make the sting of the hunk being off-limits a little less painful.

It doesn't help that I'm covered from head to toe in flour, dusted into every crevice. What man in his right mind would even be thinking about me in any sexual way with me looking more like a biscuit than a woman?

"I'm Angelo." He tips his head, just like a Southern gentleman. "I own Hook & Hustle next door with my sister and two brothers. So, I guess we're neighbors." He rubs the back of his neck, staring at my stilettos—which I wish I could wrap around his middle and see if he's as hard as he looks.

The last time I had sex was over five years ago before my husband left for a short deployment, taking off on a top-secret mission. I thought he'd come back. He always had. I'm not sure I'd even remember how sex worked at this point.

Roger keeps reminding me it's like riding a bike and not something I'd forget, but I beg to differ.

"Guess we'll be seeing a lot of each other, then."

I'm almost giddy at the possibility that I'll have at least a little eye candy to stare at every once in a while. And he said he ran the bar with his brothers, so maybe there's still hope for me, after all, since he's clearly taken.

He leans forward, wrapping his thick, strong hands around the ridiculously heavy mixer and lifting the damn thing like it weighs next to nothing.

There's something so erotic about the way he

moves. My eyes are practically glued to his biceps as they flex under the sleeves of his T-shirt.

"You make it look so easy."

"I have two kids. I'm used to lifting and carrying heavy things."

Now I've seen the ring, and he's dropped the kids straight into my lap, warning me he's totally off-limits once again.

Life can be so unfair.

It's taken me years to get to the point in my life where I feel like I'm ready for a relationship. After Mitchell passed, I never thought I'd ever be interested in another man. Now that I am, the first one to catch my eye in forever is married with kids.

"Well, I can't thank you enough for helping me."

"It was no trouble. I'm always happy to help."

Gah. He's so nice and hot. He's like the perfect combination thrown in my path just to taunt me and my very lonely vagina.

He smacks his hands together, ridding himself of the flour that's covering every surface in the kitchen, including me.

"The first batch of cupcakes is for you and your kids as a thank you."

"Don't go to all that trouble."

"I insist, Angelo."

It's the right thing to do. I was brought up to be kind and thankful for even the smallest of favors. It never hurts to make friends with a strong guy because I know my limits, and that mixer would've sat on the floor for fucking ever.

"I better go," he says, but he's not moving. He's just staring at me, and hell, I'm staring at him too.

It's all I've done since he walked through the door. A man like him is meant to be savored. God took a little extra time when he created this one, and he should be enjoyed, even if my thoughts aren't exactly holy.

"Tilly," Roger, Mitchell's older brother, calls out as he walks into the kitchen. "What in the hell happened?" His eyes roam around the kitchen and land on Angelo. "Who are you?"

"Hey, Roger. This is Angelo. The owner of the bar." My smile's tight, and I'm praying to God that Roger doesn't make a scene. He's known to be a bit overdramatic at times.

"Did you do this?" he asks Angelo like I'm not even in the room.

"Don't be silly." I wave Roger's statement away. "I dropped the mixer, and this very nice man rescued me."

Roger doesn't stop staring at Angelo. "I guess I should thank you." He doesn't finish the statement because, well, Roger's a dick.

Roger, although sweet, is a tad overbearing. He's my husband's very protective and extremely gay brother. He lords over me like I'm his girl, when he very much prefers someone like Angelo with all the proper equipment.

"Where are my manners?" I take a step between

them and place my palm against Roger's chest, but I keep my eyes locked on my new neighbor. "Angelo, this is my brother-in-law, Roger."

Angelo's eye ticks. "It's nice to meet you. Sorry to cut this short, but I have to get back to the bar." Angelo turns his gaze to me, but he's not looking at me like I'm the frosting on his favorite treat. "Let me know if you need anything, Tilly. One of us is always around, but it looks like Roger can handle whatever you need."

What I need is to get laid, and Roger most certainly cannot handle that. He told me he once had sex with a woman. It ended with him in tears, heaving because he had a hair lodged in the back of his throat. It's funny because that isn't exclusive to pussy, but the man was clearly traumatized over the event.

"Thanks!" I yell as Angelo practically runs out of the kitchen like he has fire ants biting his ass.

"Damn it," I groan, slapping Roger in the chest with the back of my hand. "You have the worst timing."

"Him?" Roger pitches his thumb over his shoulder where the swinging door is still swishing back and forth from Angelo's quick departure. "That's the type of guy you want?"

Oh, you mean sexy as fuck and strong to boot?

"No," I sigh. "He's married and has kids."

"Well then, what's the problem? Jesus, doll, you're a mess."

"Tell me something I don't already know." I start to laugh at the stupidity of the entire situation. Here I was finally stepping outside my comfort zone, coming on way too strong just like Roger had coached me, and the fucking guy is married.

To top it all off, I'm covered in flour and a complete hot mess. I wasn't even on my A game if he were single, and any chance I had at landing a hunk like that went right out the window.

"Wait, how did you drop that mixer?"

Somehow, I do the craziest shit when I'm pissed off, including tipping over an entire table because I'm a dumbass who thought it didn't need to be secured to the floor.

"Don't ask." I clear my throat. "You don't want to know."

Roger laughs and just shakes his head. "Til, if I were straight..."

"We still wouldn't happen," I remind him.

If Roger were straight, I'd crush on him hard. He's so much like Mitchell. Tough, protective, intense, and there's sweetness at his core. Even if he liked pussy, I could never look at him as anything more than a big brother. Sleeping with my husband's brother would just be...well, gross and wrong on so many levels.

I finally look down and survey the damage. There's not a patch of skin or clothes that's not covered in flour dust. It's going to take more than one shampoo to pull myself into any type of presentable. "I need a shower and a stiff drink."

"Let's get you cleaned up, and I'll take you out for

drinks. This is going to be a busy week, and you need to relax a little."

Relax? I haven't relaxed since the moment I sank every dollar I had left to my name into making my dream of owning a bakery a reality. The life insurance money from Mitchell's death made the entire thing possible, and if it fails, a small piece of him will die all over again.

"I know just the place." I waggle my eyebrows.

HOURS later and an entire bottle of shampoo down, Roger and I walk into Hook & Hustle. The sun's just starting to set in the city, creating the most magnificent shadows on the sidewalks of the old neighborhood. The pavement is covered with a fresh sheet of snow, sparkling like a million little diamonds from the overhead lights lining the street.

"Well," Roger says as soon as we step inside the bar. "It's not upscale."

The man's all about things being nice, and he prefers to hang out on the North Side or in Boys Town, neither of which has ever been my cup of tea.

Hook & Hustle is the quintessential neighborhood bar. Dark and warm, brimming with people and lively conversation.

"I have a good feeling about this place." I spot an empty booth and grab his hand. "Come on, stick in the mud. Try to have a little fun tonight. Maybe smile a little bit. Never know, you may find the love of your life in here."

We slide into the booth, and Roger glances around. "Doesn't look like there's a gay man in the place, Til. Look at them." He waves his hand in the direction of the customers sitting around the bar. "What do you see?"

I study them, taking in their flannel shirts and casual clothing, the exact opposite of Roger and me. "I see possibility." I give him a wink.

Roger's lips purse. "I see blue-collar straight men and nothing else."

"Exactly." I smile. "This night is about me, not you."

"What can I get ya?" a woman asks, holding no less than six empty beer bottles in her hands.

"Tequila on the rocks, no salt."

Roger dips his head, knowing I'm about to turn it up a notch or make a scene before the night's through. "What type of craft beers do you have on tap?"

She rattles off a list before Roger finally makes his selection. The man is beyond picky.

"Beer is beer," I tell him as soon as she walks away. "For fuck's sake, you make everything so complicated."

"I don't put trash in my mouth, doll. That goes for beer and cocks."

I stare across the table at Roger and smirk. "What about Harvey?"

He winces, hating to be reminded of the time he

slummed it for about a month with a roughneck welder from the South Side. "He was a lapse in judgment." Roger taps his fingers against the table as he glances out the window, avoiding all eye contact and putting an end to our Harvey conversation. He's so finicky when it comes to men.

Between my inability to move on after his brother and his weirdo obsession with finding the perfect creature, we're both doomed to be single forever.

"Tequila on the rocks, no salt," the waitress says as she places my drink on the table before turning her attention toward Roger. "And your beer."

"Is Angelo here?" I blurt out before she has a chance to walk away.

"He left. He works the day shift mostly."

"Makes sense with the wife and kids." Roger lifts the beer toward his lips, eyeing me over the rim. He likes to twist the knife, knowing I'm pining over someone I can't have.

Maybe that's why I like Angelo.

He's unavailable.

Kind of like my heart.

"No wife," the woman tells us. "She passed a few years back from cancer, but my niece and nephew need their daddy at night."

My eyes widen, and there's an ache deep in my chest, knowing the amount of pain Angelo must've endured. "I'm so sorry."

"Life's a bitch, right?"

"I'm Tilly." I hold out my hand. "I'm opening the cupcake shop next door. I met Angelo earlier, and he told me he ran the bar with his siblings."

"Daphne." She shakes my hand. "Our brother Lucio is around here somewhere, but Vinnie's away at college, so you'll barely see him."

She is absolutely beautiful, just like her brother. The genes in this family run deep.

"My parents live above the bar, so even if we're closed, don't hesitate to knock if you need something."

"How quaint," Roger murmurs against his glass.

"Need anything else?" She eyes Roger and the sweater he has draped over his shoulders like he just walked out of the latest issue of *GQ*.

"We're good, Daphne. Thanks."

As soon as we're alone, Roger gives me a look.

"What?" I shrug.

"He's single."

"He's widowed," I remind him. "There's a difference."

Being single by choice makes dating easier than being robbed of love.

"So are you," he reminds me.

Like I could've forgotten. But Mitchell's death is always there, hanging over my shoulders just like Roger's ridiculous sweater.

"He still wears his ring."

Roger raises an eyebrow. "And?"

"He's not ready." I shake my head.

It took me years before I could remove my wedding band after Mitchell died. I sobbed the day I finally tucked it away for safekeeping, trying to put my past behind me so I could move forward. I felt like I was betraying his memory, but it was my first step in the rest of my life.

Although Mitchell had taken his last breath, I still had a life to live even if I couldn't imagine going on without him.

CHAPTER FOUR

ANGELO

"THE CUPCAKE CHICK was looking for you last night." Daphne gives me a shitty smirk from across the dinner table.

"Cupcake chick?" Ma asks, glancing between the two of us and giving Daphne the reaction she wanted.

"You know, Ma. The new store opening next to the bar." Daphne's still staring at me, wanting to open a can of worms that isn't even there. "She asked for you."

"Daphne, don't make it something it isn't."

"She looks mighty sweet too," she adds, twisting that knife a little deeper in my gut.

"Is she single?" my ma asks.

"Stop," I growl.

These two are always willing to cook up some scheme if it involves me finding a new wife.

"I don't know. She was in the bar with some guy."

"Roger," I grumble.

Daphne gasps. "I knew you were interested."

I stab at the overcooked potato, ignoring my sister's comment because I don't know what the hell I am. I wouldn't say I was interested. I met her for a total of five minutes, and I probably wouldn't recognize her if I walked by her on the street and she wasn't covered in flour.

"She needed help, and I was just being kind."

Daphne eyes me. "Mm-hm."

I lean back, placing my fork on my plate, and stare my sister down. "Don't get any ideas in that hormonal brain of yours."

"It's time."

"I agree with your sister." Ma's trying to outvote me on something neither of them has any say in.

"What's wrong?" Lucio asks, finally getting his head out of his ass to save me.

"Your brother met a girl." Ma overstates what really happened, which is usually the case.

The entire table of people goes quiet and turns in my direction. There's nothing I hate more in life than being the center of attention.

"That's fabulous news." Delilah claps her hands, way too enthusiastic for me.

"I haven't met anyone. Jesus." I push back from the

table, about to stalk out of the room, when Lucio grabs my arm.

"Sit," Lucio tells me as he narrows his eyes. "Don't be a pussy."

For a moment, I think about punching him in the face, but I decide to act like a grown-up and sit back down. "Are you taking my side?"

"There are no sides. Everyone around this table wants the best for you. Now, what's going on?" He pats my arm before he finally releases me.

I take a deep breath and crack my neck, trying to relieve some of the stress that's always weighing on my shoulders. "Honestly?"

He nods.

"Nothing. The lady next door dropped something, and I helped her pick it up. That's all."

"Is she cute?" he asks.

"She's all right." I'm lying. From the little bit I could see underneath all that flour, she was cute as fuck.

"Hmm." He rubs the scruff on his chin. "So, just okay?"

Daphne rolls her eyes. "Lame."

"She was covered head to toe in flour, but from what I could see, she wasn't bad-looking."

"Oh, she's cute, all right," Daphne chimes in. "She's just your type."

I grind my teeth together. "I don't have a type."

"You're so precious." The shitty smirk's back on Daphne's face. "You most certainly *do* have a type."

"Why don't you enlighten me?" I lean back, sliding my arm behind my mother's chair, and wait for Daphne to impart her wisdom to the entire family. She thinks she knows everything about me, but she's wrong.

Daphne pushes her plate forward and gives herself a little room. "Well…" She waves her hand. "You like your ladies more on the adorable, innocent-looking side than the sex-kitten type."

"Sweet Jesus," Ma mumbles.

"You want the type that looks like they can teach Sunday school."

"You're insane."

"No. No." Daphne shakes her head. "It's your thing."

"I think it's a lot of guys' *thing*." Leo earns himself a slap to the chest with that statement.

"Shut it," she tells him, giving him the side-eye. "You married me."

"I didn't say it was my type, *bella*." He grabs her hand and lifts it to his mouth, turning on the Casanova charm that won her over in the first place.

"Even though you like the pure-as-the-driven-snow look, you also like a woman with a dirty mouth."

"It's hot." Lucio nods his head slowly and wraps one arm around Delilah. "This one can swear like a sailor."

Delilah blushes and rests her head on his shoulder. They're so stinking cute, they make me a little sick with all their adorableness.

"Anyway," Daphne continues, ignoring Lucio and

Delilah as they fawn over each other. "You also go for the chicks who are a little broken."

"Seriously, Dee, you're describing every man on the planet here." I wave off her insanity.

"I'm not." She looks at Leo. "He doesn't want innocent, and I was never broken or in need of help."

"If I remember correctly, you were about to face-plant in front of three hundred wedding guests when I saved you." The look Leo gets from my sister is one I can only describe as lethal.

"And you want the woman to be just as sweet on the inside as she looks on the out. If we weren't brother and sister, we'd never work. I'm too bitchy and bossy for you."

"Your lips to God's ears," Leo whispers and glances up at the ceiling.

"Every man wants a good woman at their side." Pop places his hand over my mother's. "Without her, we'd be lost."

And that's exactly where I am.

Lost.

Without Marissa, I feel like I'm just wandering through life. Even when Michelle and I would hang out, the sadness wouldn't leave my soul. She didn't fill up my heart the way a woman should, or at least, the way Marissa did. I'm not sure there's anyone in the world who could fill the void her death has left.

"Hello. You're forgetting about Roger," I remind my sister and the entire family.

"She's not in love with him." She shakes her head because, clearly, she knows way more than I do about a total stranger.

"You don't know that."

"If I'm in love with the man I'm having a drink with, I most certainly do not ask for another man."

"Maybe she just wanted to say thank you," I tell her.

"Nope. She had herself all dolled up. She was there with a purpose."

"Daphne, I love you, but you're off your rocker."

"Daddy," Tate says from the archway to the kitchen. "Can you help me?"

"I'm coming, baby." I push back from the table, thankful Tate's saving me. "This conversation's over."

"Mark my words…" Daphne says as I walk out of the room, but I don't stop to hear the end of the statement.

———

"WATCH, DADDY." Tate pushes off the cinder blocks in the alley, showing me how well she can ride her bike without training wheels. She has the biggest smile on her face as the bike wobbles back and forth, but she doesn't stop peddling. Even though it snowed last night, most has melted due to the unusually sunny winter day.

"Good job, baby!" I'm a little choked up, but my voice doesn't waver. Something this small and trivial shouldn't evoke this much emotion, but it's another step in her growing up and another thing Marissa has missed.

"She's growing up fast." Ma walks outside and joins me behind the bar. "Soon, she'll be dating and going away to college."

"Ma, come on. She's in elementary school." I wave to Tate as she glides by, a little steadier this time.

"Look, Grandma." Tate smiles, but her eyes are quickly forced back on the path when the handlebars start to turn.

"You're doing good, sweetheart." Ma claps as Tate speeds by.

"Angelo, I remember being out here with you when you were her age. It feels like yesterday. It all went by in the blink of an eye."

"Time doesn't pass so fast for me, Ma," I confess. Every day since Marissa died has felt like a year, passing ever so torturously slow.

Ma wraps her arm around my middle and places her head on my arm. "Now that Michelle's gone, it's time for you to move forward. That was fun while it lasted, but you need to get serious about your future."

Jesus. "I liked Michelle, Ma, but…"

"She wasn't the right one, baby. It's okay to scratch an itch with someone you trust. That's just being a man and alive."

"I shouldn't have."

"Oh, stop. You're still breathing, Angelo. A man has needs."

I glance down at her. "Ma, can we change the subject?"

"Fine. I won't talk about sex." She grips my waist tighter.

"Thank fuck," I whisper.

"Let's talk about the cupcake."

And just like clockwork, Tilly walks out of the back of her store and steps into the alley. She's bathed in sunlight, looking so damn angelic and more beautiful than I ever could've imagined underneath the sea of white she was wearing when we met.

"Wow," Ma says exactly what I'm thinking. "I take it that's her?"

"Angelo!" Tilly waves with one hand and shields her eyes with the other.

I wave back, careful not to be overenthusiastic, even though my stomach does this weird thing when I let my eyes travel down her body. She's wearing a black pencil skirt that goes down past her knees, a white blouse with the first two buttons undone, and red stiletto heels that accentuate the muscles in her legs.

I suck in a breath as she saunters our way, feeling like I've taken a punch to the gut. Her brown hair looks more auburn in the sun, with streaks of red and orange blazing through the brown.

"Hi." She looks at my mom as she gets closer, and she pulls her black knee-length coat closed. "I'm Tilly. I'm opening the cupcake shop."

My mother holds out her hand to Tilly but keeps the

other one securely fastened around my waist. "I'm Betty, Angelo's mother."

Tilly shakes my mother's hand, but her eyes are locked on me for a few seconds before she speaks. "It's wonderful to meet you, Betty."

The deep sea of green in her eyes is striking, almost changing by the second in the daylight.

"You as well." I can hear the happiness in my ma's voice.

"Daddy!" Tate draws my attention back to the cupcake standing in front of me. "Look." Tate lifts one hand off the handlebar, tempting fate.

"Hold on, baby." I shake my head, but I stop myself from running down the alley and snatching her off the bike. "Don't play around."

"She's a brave little thing, isn't she?" Tilly asks.

"She's too much like her mother. She's going to be the death of me."

Tilly laughs, and it's the most glorious sound in the world. "That's a little girl's job."

I lift an eyebrow. "Killing their fathers?"

"No. Keeping life interesting."

"I better get inside and check on your father. It was wonderful meeting you, Tilly. Don't be a stranger." Ma glances up at me and winks. "Take your time."

I'm not sure if she's talking about Tate riding her bike or letting Tilly into my world. "We'll be up for dessert."

"You're more than welcome to join us, Tilly," Ma

offers, taking a page out of my sister's book. Always nosy and looking for an angle.

"That's mighty sweet, but I have a batch of cupcakes I just put in the oven. I can't leave them. I'm testing a new recipe."

"I'm a good taste tester but an awful cook, dear. If you ever need help or a willing mouth, I'm always around." Ma releases me and steps backward. "And so is Angelo."

Tilly blushes and can't hide her smile. "Thank you, ma'am."

"Betty, dear. Betty."

"Thanks, Betty," Tilly says before my mother steps back into the bar, leaving us alone.

"So." I tuck my hands into my pockets like I'm sixteen again and totally unsure of what the hell to say to a girl.

"I want to apologize for yesterday."

My eyebrows shoot up. "Apologize? For what?"

"I came on a little strong, and that's totally not me."

"I didn't think you were coming on strong." I'm being nice, of course. She was coming on strong, but I'd be lying if I said I didn't like it.

"Oh, please." She touches my arm, sending little shock waves up and down my skin. "I was acting like a…"

"You were sweet." I do nothing to pull away from her touch.

She's standing so close, and all I can smell is vanilla

and everything cake. "I've been trying to step outside my comfort zone, and I may have gone a little over the top." She laughs and does this adorable thing with her head. "Okay, maybe a lot over the top. I don't want you to think I'm a lunatic or a harlot."

"It's been a long time since I've heard someone say harlot." I give her a dopey smile, and my insides warm despite the cold breeze.

"It's a Southern thing. I grew up in a tiny town in Georgia. You can take the girl out of the South, but you can't take the South out of the girl."

"How did you end up here?"

"My husband was stationed at Great Lakes. He was a Navy SEAL and was an instructor for a bit, training new recruits."

"Oh."

"When he died, I didn't know where else to go. My parents passed years ago, and I had no family back in Georgia anymore. I stayed because of my brother-in-law, Roger."

"I'm sorry," I say, familiar with the pain she felt. "I know how hard it is to lose your spouse."

She gives me a pained smile and tightens her grip on my arm. "I heard about your wife. I'm so sorry, Angelo. No one should have to endure the kind of heartache we have."

I place my hand over hers, allowing myself a moment to grieve and take solace in a stranger. "No, they shouldn't, Tilly."

"Hi, I'm Tate." Tate practically pushes her way between us.

I drag my eyes away from Tilly, almost forgetting that Tate was riding her bike back and forth, probably watching me like a hawk. "Hey, baby."

"Hi, Tate. I'm Tilly. I own the cupcake shop."

Tate's eyes go wide. "I love cupcakes," she whispers. "Are you my daddy's new friend?"

"I think so." Tilly peers up at me.

"Tate, Tilly and I just met."

"Daddy," Tate almost sings my name. "Remember our talk the other night?"

"Tate."

"She's perfect." Tate nods quickly.

Tilly blushes, probably able to guess what we're talking about. I'm a little mortified that my kid is throwing me under the bus just like everyone else in my damn family.

"Go ride your bike." I tap her cute little nose.

"My daddy's getting me a horse," Tate tells Tilly, being defiant and not listening to me.

"Really?" Tilly crouches down, getting eye-to-eye with Tate, and somehow keeps her balance on those ridiculous shoes.

"Yeah." Tate twists her little body back and forth. "Auntie Nee said he needs to get back in the saddle."

Tilly laughs loudly, covering her mouth with her hand, and she glances up at me. "Well, I don't…"

I shake my head because I'm not ready to crush

Tate's dreams just yet. "We'll talk about it later, Tate. You have five minutes before dessert."

Tate reaches over and grabs Tilly's hand away from her face, pulling her toward her bike lying on the ground. "Let me show you my bike, Cupcake."

"It's Tilly," I remind her because she knows better.

"It's fine." Tilly winks. "I kind of like it."

I thought I was fucked when I saw her covered in flour, swearing like she could give lessons in profanity. But now...watching Tate walk away hand in hand with another woman, and seeing a genuine smile on Tate's face for the first time in years, I know I'm double fucked.

CHAPTER FIVE

TILLY

"ARE YOU CRYING?" Roger walks into the kitchen, catching me wiping the tears away from my face.

Wine and baking do not mix. After running into Angelo and Tate, I cracked open a bottle and decided it was a splendid idea to drown my sorrows.

"Grab an apron and stop judging." I scrape the sides of the mixing bowl as tears stream down my face.

"Tilly." He touches my elbow, trying to comfort me, but I'm too far gone, and honestly, too tipsy for anything to get through. "What happened?"

I turn to face him with the spatula in my hand, dripping with chocolate cupcake batter. This isn't my finest moment, but it's raw and real. "I met his kid, Roger."

The space between his eyebrows wrinkles. "Whose kid?"

"Angelo's, and she's precious. Completely adorable. You should've seen her."

My face is doing this weird thing. A cross between a smile and an ugly cry. By the look on Roger's face, it's painful to look at and not pretty.

"That's nice," he says, like we're talking about the weather.

"Nice?"

He drops his hand from my elbow and rubs the back of his neck. "Well, yeah. What else should I say?"

I shake my head and grab my wine, needing just one more sip. I don't know how to explain all the emotions I'm feeling after meeting Tate and seeing the way Angelo is with her. It's heartwarming and heartbreaking all at the same time.

Before I can bring the glass to my lips, Roger tries to snatch the damn thing from my hands, but I twist in the opposite direction. "I think you should slow down."

I'm careful not to spill a drop and level him with my glare. "You are not my father."

I hate being handled, especially by Roger. While he means well, the last thing I need is for him to tell me what to do or how to feel. I had months of that after Mitchell died. Between the counselors, military wives, and Roger, I had had enough.

He lifts his hands in the air. "Point taken."

"Either join me in a drink, or you know where the

door is." I lift my chin, defiant and petulant as I take a sip.

Roger grabs the wineglass I set out for him, filling it to the top without even looking at me. "So, tell me about the kid. What has you so…"

He's walking on eggshells. He wants to say crazy, but it's a term he knows will make me come unglued. I'm not insane. I'm emotional.

Fuck, I'm grieving.

Anyone who's been through losing a spouse will know the insanity that follows. Emotions change quicker than the direction of the wind, and there's no warning before the anger suddenly strikes or the sadness becomes unbearable.

"I'm feeling so many things."

Roger nods but doesn't speak. He's learned it's best to say as little as possible and let me blabber on. It took months for him to realize I just need someone to listen to me.

"I look at her little face and imagine what it would be like to have a little piece of Mitchell here with me."

"Oh," Roger whispers, deciding it's time to start drinking the wine he's holding.

I begin to pace, kicking off my shoes because my feet are freaking killing me. "Then I think, why would I want to put the sadness I feel in my bones on someone so young and innocent."

I chug half the glass before I speak again. "Tate took my hand today and wanted nothing more than to show me her bike. She kept looping her finger through my hair as I bent down to check out the pink paint and her cute little white basket."

The tears come a little faster this time because my heart ached from the moment she touched me. I wanted to wrap her in my arms and never let go. No child should feel the pain of love and loss at such a young age. I was in college when my mother died, and it damn near broke me.

Roger hops up on the steel table and watches me, staying silent and nodding his head.

"I don't know how Angelo does it," I say and then stop moving, looking over at Roger. "I don't know how he got this far. How can you grieve and raise two kids?"

"I don't know. I remember you wouldn't even get out of bed for a month, and then…"

"I know. I felt and smelled like trash." It wasn't my proudest moment, but it was all I could do. I wanted to curl up and die, joining Mitchell wherever he was. "I was so in shock, I barely remember that month, honestly."

"You were literally a day away from the county mental ward."

I stalk across the tile floor in my bare feet and look him straight in the eye. "They never would've taken me alive."

"That's why I never called. I wasn't willing to lose you. Not after losing Mitchell."

I can see the pain in his eyes. Sometimes I'm so lost

in my grief, I forget he lost his only sibling. He became an only child in a heartbeat, just like I'd become a widow.

He opens his legs as I move closer. "Why did this happen, Roger?" I place my head in the middle of his chest. "Why?"

He sets his wineglass next to his legs before prying my glass from my hands. "There's no reason, Til. Life doesn't make sense sometimes."

I peer up, eyes filled with tears. "I need things to make sense."

He touches my chin. "I don't know if life will ever be normal or that we'll ever get the answers we want."

Five years later and the government is still investigating Mitchell's missions, trying to figure out what went so terribly wrong. My husband wasn't the only casualty that day. He was one of five brave SEALs tasked with rescuing American hostages behind enemy lines.

"Answers won't change anything," I whisper and drop my head back against his chest.

He wraps his arms around my body, rubbing my back. He's warm and smells amazing, just like his brother used to. "Nothing will take away the sadness. The only thing we can do is go on and try to find a new happiness."

I twist his shirt between my fingers, using the cloth as a tissue for my tears. "I'm trying."

Roger grumbles, hating when I ruin his clothes with

my snot, but he doesn't chastise me. "You see your pain in Angelo, don't you?"

"I see a different kind of pain, Roger. One that may be more profound. Scars that run deep."

"What do you mean?"

I keep my face planted in his chest, finding it easier to talk when I don't have to look at him. I close my eyes and take a deep breath before I try explaining what's going on in my head. "His wife died of cancer."

"Okay."

"When Mitchell died, it was a shock. Everything changed in a single second, you know?"

"I do." He blows out a breath, probably remembering when the Navy showed up at my front door.

I was the one who had to tell Roger about his brother. I was notified first since I was his wife and legally his next of kin. Showing up at Roger's door, having to tell him his only brother was gone was more than my heart could bear. Saying the words made it real, and I wasn't ready for what would follow.

"Angelo lived in hell for months before she died, Roger. You know how cancer works. Treatments, doctors, chemo, and everything that goes along with trying to survive."

"I know all too well."

Roger's best friend died of cancer two years ago, and the toll on him was immense. I remember watching him struggle to hold it together, going through the grief that still hadn't healed from Mitchell.

"I wish I could've said goodbye to Mitchell. I wish I could've had time with him to say everything that needed to be said. Angelo had that. But he had to endure the months of watching his wife die slowly before his eyes."

"Oh, Tilly," Roger whispers against the top of my hair as he holds me tighter. "You can't compare grief and loss."

He's right. Grief is grief. There's no easy way to do it. There's no one way better than another. But there're things I wished I'd said to my husband that I'll never be able to say.

Roger's hands cup my face, forcing me to look at him. "The one thing I know is my brother loved you. There wasn't anything you could've said to him that he didn't already know."

"You're right, but that doesn't make it easier."

Roger brushes my damp hair away from my face. "I went through the slow process of dying with Chet, baby. I don't know if I could've done that with Mitchell. I couldn't have sat there, day after day, seeing him dying and knowing there was nothing I could do." Roger closes his eyes, and I can hear the emotion in his voice. "Mitchell left us doing what he loved. He was born to be a military man. He was a fighter and one of the damn best there was too. He'd want us to celebrate his life, and he for damn sure wouldn't want you alone forever."

"I don't know if I could leave this world and tell him to move on without me. I'm not that nice of a person,

Roger. I'd be haunting his ass from the great beyond if he ever laid his hands on another woman."

Roger laughs and shakes his head. "I have no doubt you'd be relentless."

"I like Angelo," I whisper like I'm confessing a sin. "I feel guilty saying those words too."

"You two are tied in grief. You've experienced something very few people have at your age. It's only natural you're going to be drawn to him."

"But I'm not just drawn to him because of the pain." I hate saying those words out loud. I feel guilty wanting another person or feeling the almost forgotten flicker of lust.

"He's hot if you like that look." Roger makes a face.

"You mean hot? He's such a hardship on the eyes."

"He's a little rough around the edges for me."

"Well then, it's a good thing he doesn't like dick." I laugh, feeling like a weight has been lifted off my shoulders after having this talk with Roger.

"He'd totally be a top if he did, and that would be a problem."

"I'll never understand gay men."

"I'll never understand women, so we're even." He laughs. "Now what is all this mess?" He waves his hand around the kitchen, which doesn't look all that much cleaner since I had the flour bomb.

"I'm making a special cupcake for Tate."

"You're a goner, kid," he says, and I totally agree.

CHAPTER SIX

ANGELO

"Why are the kids off school today?" Pop asks as he walks into the bar around noon.

"It's spring break, Pop."

"For fuck's sake. How long do these kids need?" He runs his hand down the side of his head, smoothing his salt-and-pepper hair. "When I was a kid…"

"Did they have school that long ago?" I get in a jab whenever possible because he's earned as much.

"I'm pretty sure they used stone tablets back then," Lucio chimes in, yanking my father's chain.

"You two can fuck right off."

"What are Tate and Brax doing?" I ask, not hearing a peep from upstairs.

Usually, when they're quiet, it means they're sleeping or getting into trouble. The older they get, the more damage they create.

"Brax is playing dinosaurs in the kitchen, and Tate is showing your mother how to use her iPad."

"Sweet baby Jesus," Lucio mutters. "It's been years, and she still has no freaking clue how to use that damn thing."

"Ma still listens to music on vinyl."

Lucio and I laugh.

Pop gives us the side-eye. "Music sounds better on a record," he says, coming to her defense.

"For sure." Lucio elbows me. "I hate that we stopped using the 8-tracks. That was where it was at."

"So, what's up with the chick next door?" Pop ticks his head toward the adjoining wall. "Your mother had a lot to say about her last night, but then again, she has a lot to say about everyone."

"There's nothing up with the chick next door."

My tone's a little defensive. I can hear it in my voice. I'm not fooling anyone either.

Lucio levels me with his gaze. "Don't be an asshole, and stop lying to us and yourself."

"I've met the woman twice. That does not constitute anything going on."

Lucio crosses his arms. "Do you like her?"

I shrug as I busy myself cleaning the bar top before we officially open the doors for business. "I don't know."

Do I like her?

Lucio slides his hands under his shirt and lifts his fingers, replicating a heartbeat. "Does she make your heart do this funny thing in your chest?"

"We're not having this conversation."

"Does she make your junk feel alive again?" he continues, but I'm not playing along.

Pop comes to sit on a barstool near where I'm cleaning. I can feel the weight of his stare without looking up. "I know I'm not the best person to talk to about this shit, but the one thing I know a lot about is wasted time. There's nothing worse than looking back and realizing everything you missed."

"Spoken like a man with regret," Lucio mutters under his breath.

"I have many regrets," Pop tells him, hearing his words clear as a bell. "I regret all the years I missed with you kids. I regret the holidays and evenings I missed with your mother in my arms. I missed out on way too much. More than a person should miss in a lifetime. But I made my bed."

"I have too many regrets, too."

Mine all are about Marissa. The countless hours I spent at the bar when I should've been home with her. Precious seconds I wasted, thinking there would always be more, when that wasn't the case.

"The only thing you can do is move forward and try not to repeat the mistakes of the past."

Who is this man? Where did my father go? He's

never been one to dole out words of wisdom, and even when he did, they were never any good.

"For once, I can finally agree with Pop on something," Lucio says, shocking both of us.

"Helloooo," a woman says from the doorway. "Are you open?"

I'd know that voice anywhere. Tilly's twang is like music to my ears after listening to them prattle on about what I should do with my life.

"Well, come on in, doll. It's cold outside." Pop motions to her as he glances in our direction.

"I just wanted to drop these off for Tate." Tilly's bathed in sunlight, looking like an angel and holding a pink box in one hand.

Lucio leans over. "Dude, she's gorgeous."

"Shut up," I whisper, but he's absolutely right. The woman is off the charts beautiful.

"And she bakes. Don't be a dumb fuck," he tells me as Tilly heads toward us.

My father's on his feet quickly and cuts her off before she can make it to the bar. "I'm Santino, their father."

"It's nice to meet you, Santino. I'm Tilly Carter, owner of the cupcake shop next door."

My father grabs her free hand and brings it to his lips. "Well, it's a pleasure to meet such a fine woman."

Tilly blushes and lets out a small laugh. "You're a handsome devil, aren't you? I see where your boys get their good looks."

Pop is eating up the compliments. He stands a little straighter, probably as sucked in by her beauty as I am. I can't let him linger, and I head their way, cutting him off before he has a chance to sweet-talk her a little more.

"Go get her," Lucio says quietly, just as annoying as my sister and mother.

The silly thing Lucio did with his hands under his shirt earlier rang true. My heart speeds up, beating a little harder and stronger than it was moments before she walked through the door.

Everything about Tilly Carter is sheer and utter perfection—from her pert little nose, light freckles dotting her round, high cheeks, and wavy auburn hair that changes color like the weather.

"Well, aren't you a sweet little thing." Pop holds his hand out, forcing Tilly backward a little so he can get another look.

I know he's soaking her in, and it's easy to do with the outfit she has on underneath that knee-length coat. The woman probably doesn't own a pair of jeans or sweat pants. I've only seen her in pencil skirts and blouses, looking like she's about to go out to dinner at a fancy restaurant instead of whipping up a new batch of desserts.

"Easy now." I place my hand on my father's shoulder because he's overreaching.

Maybe that was a part of his plan. We're a lot like him. We don't share, especially when it comes to women. We stake our claim, stand our ground, and defend what we feel is ours, even from family.

Tilly pulls her bottom lip into her mouth, biting down with her teeth. Fuck. Her eyes sparkle as they travel up my body, looking hungry. "Hey," she says softly.

"Hey, yourself." Butterflies the likes of which I haven't felt in years fill my insides.

"Lame," Lucio whispers from across the bar, and I flip him off behind my back so only he can see.

But he's right. I am lame. I'm like an awkward teenager, suddenly unsure and timid.

Tilly thrusts the open pink box in my direction. "I made these for Tate."

I glance down at the dozen or so perfect little pink-frosted cupcakes covered in multicolored glitter.

"They're my mermaid special. I created them just for her."

I'm a little speechless at the thoughtfulness and time she took in creating what I'm sure is no doubt the most delicious thing I'll ever eat. "You shouldn't have." I peer up, meeting her gaze.

"It was no trouble. I just whipped up a little something."

I like that she understates everything.

"Want me to get Tate?" Pop asks.

"Sure," I say, unable to take my eyes off the woman standing in front of me.

I barely notice him walk away or the sound of his

footsteps on the stairs leading up to their place. I'm too transfixed by Tilly. We're staring at each other, not saying a word, but there's nothing awkward about the lack of talking.

I want to touch her, but I don't. I already know she could very well be dangerous to my heart, and I haven't even laid a hand on her. I'm pretty sure one touch or taste would be all I'd need to be a goner forever.

"Tilly," Tate screeches as she runs down the stairs and straight toward Tilly and the box of cupcakes.

"Hey, princess." Tilly crouches down to Tate's level.

Tate's eyes widen. "They're so pretty."

"I made them just for you." Tilly lifts the box closer to Tate's face. "They're my Tate's Mermaid Special."

Tate's mouth drops open. "They're all mine?"

"You have to share with your brother," I tell her because she'd lord those over Brax's head until the little guy cried. The last thing I want is a sugar-high daughter and a whiny little boy all evening.

She lifts her finger high in the air, not bothering to look at me because she's too taken with all the goodness in front of her. "He can have one. Only one," she tells me.

I glance upward, not sure if I should laugh or dread the bossy little thing she's become. "You can't eat them all."

"They're mine. Tilly said so." Tate scrunches up her face.

This girl is seriously going to be the death of me. I

already know, as she gets older, her attitude's only going to get worse. Everyone keeps telling me to enjoy her now because all hell's going to break loose as soon as she hits puberty. I'm dreading those years.

Tilly peers up at me and mouths, "I'm sorry."

"Don't be," I tell her and crouch down with them.

"I thought she deserved a treat after she was so kind to me yesterday."

"Tilly," my mother says, coming down the stairs with Brax at her side. "It's so wonderful to see you again, my dear."

"Hi, Betty," Tilly replies.

Somehow, a regular shift at the bar has turned into a family affair. I'll never hear the end of this either. I know everyone is going to be on my back until I act. I gave Lucio enough shit about Delilah when he wasn't sure what to do, and my brother's all about payback.

"Cupcakes!" Brax yells and runs toward Tilly.

Tate snatches the box from her hands and turns away from him. "They're mine, Brax."

"Tate," I warn, but what the hell am I going to do? These are the times when I wish Marissa were around because the two of them together can be more than a handful.

"Now, Tate. Share with your brother. What fun is a treat if you can't share it with someone special?" Tilly touches Tate's pudgy cheek. "I'll make you more."

"Do I have to?" Tate's shoulders slump forward.

"How about this..." Tilly looks up at me, but I'm

letting her roll wherever she's going. "If you share with your brother, you can come to the shop whenever you want and pick out a cupcake."

"Every day?" Tate asks because the kid is a bottomless pit when it comes to anything sweet. She's smart too. She's hedging her bets and making sure there's a payoff for her somewhere.

Tilly laughs, looking up at me. "As often as your daddy allows."

"Any cupcake?"

"Any cupcake you want," Tilly tells her.

I can see the war going on in Tate's head. She doesn't want to share, but the prospect of unlimited future cupcakes is tempting to any child.

"Fine," she whispers and turns her body so Brax can reach a cupcake. "I'll share."

"You can each have one," I tell them, knowing the quiet that my mother was enjoying is about to come to an end because the sugar high is going to be extreme.

"Would you like to come up for a coffee?" Ma comes to stand next to us. "I'm watching the kids while the boys get the bar ready for service."

Tilly looks at me. Why? I don't know. It's not my place to tell her what to do or where she can go. Even if she were mine, I wouldn't dare stop her from doing something she wanted.

I know my mother is going to pry, feeling Tilly out and seeing if there's any hope for us. That's what she does. One thing about Betty Gallo is she is the master of manipulation with a dash of interrogation.

"I'd love that, Betty."

Poor Tilly. She has no idea what she's getting herself into, but she's about to find out. I just pray my mother doesn't come on too strong or declare my intentions when I'm not so sure what they even are at this point.

"Yay!" Tate jumps straight up, almost knocking every cupcake out of the box. "Tilly's coming over."

"Twilly!" Brax joins in on the excitement.

"Daddy." Tate bumps me with her behind. "You want a cupcake?" She hoists the box above her head, offering me one.

"I'm good, baby. You go upstairs with Grandma and Tilly and enjoy *one* cupcake."

"Two," she argues and bats her eyelashes.

"Tate." I know it's a losing battle. My mother is going to give the kids whatever she wants, no matter what I say. She always does.

"Come on, sweetheart. Don't you worry about your daddy." Ma ushers Tate toward the stairwell with a devilish grin. "Let's us girls, and Brax too, have some cupcakes and milk. We have much to discuss."

Tilly peers over her shoulder at me as she follows my mother to the stairs, and she looks a little like a deer in headlights. I can't stop myself from smiling, trying to make her feel better about the interrogation I have no doubt is about to happen.

CHAPTER SEVEN

TILLY

"Let's have a little chat, shall we?" I glare. "You're going to stop being such a pain in my ass and do as you're told."

"Dear?"

I freeze, staring at the fancy cappuccino machine I just gave a good talking-to. I'm sure I look like a lunatic. I'm talking to an inanimate object, giving it the business like it's actually going to listen.

I turn and plaster a smile on my face, hoping Betty didn't actually hear my crazy conversation. "Hey, Betty."

She's smiling. That's a good sign. Or she already thinks I'm nuts, and I've just confirmed every thought she has about me. "Having problems?"

My shoulders sag forward as I groan. "This damn

machine. I don't know why I thought it was a good idea to get such a complicated contraption."

Betty laughs as she steps into the middle of the shop. "I'm sure Angelo can figure it out," she says.

"Maybe I'll ask him for help."

"He loves helping."

She's selling him hard. She doesn't have to with me. I already know he's a diamond in the rough. The way he treats his kids makes my empty womb crave to be filled.

"The shop's coming along nicely." She glances around. "I'd guess you like pink."

"Eh," I mutter. "I'm more of a red girl, but that's a little too jarring for a cupcake place."

"Who said?"

"The designer I hired. She said pink and cream are more inviting. She gave me the psychology behind the color theory, but for the life of me, I can't remember. Anyway, is there something I can help you with?"

"I wanted to talk about earlier." She pulls the gloves off her hands and keeps her eyes on me. "I hope you didn't think I was being too pushy."

"I'd never think that."

She was forward, but her honesty was a breath of fresh air. I always get Roger's opinion, but since he has a penis, his opinion isn't always on point.

"Why don't I grab us two drinks from the bar, and we can finish our chat?"

"How about some cocoa instead? I still have so

much work to do. If I start drinking, I'm going to end up in bed way earlier than I want."

"Cocoa, it is." She slides into the pink velvet banquette I had specially made for the shop and places her gloves on the tabletop.

"I'll be right back," I tell her before I head into the kitchen to grab two mugs and the cocoa I'd been heating on the stove.

Even though I've been in Chicago for years, my body hasn't gotten used to the cold. Growing up in the South, anything below sixty was enough to cause my body to go into shock. Cocoa had become my staple to get me through the cold winter nights, especially since Mitchell died.

"Here we go." I take the seat across from her and place the two mugs in front of us.

She wraps her slender fingers around the mug, soaking in the warmth. "When's the grand opening again?"

"In a week." I sigh. "I'm so far behind, and my contractor is a flake."

"That's a shame."

I shrug. I've learned not to depend on anyone, even when money's involved. "I should've planned for this, but I was too caught up in the excitement, I didn't have a backup plan."

She lifts the mug to her lips and blows across the top. "It's hard to plan for the unexpected sometimes."

Isn't that the truth? I never expected Mitchell not to

come back from his mission. When we married, I knew what kind of life I was getting myself into. Military life isn't for everyone. I accepted his long absences because he always came back to me. I knew he was in danger every time he went off to God knows where, but never once did I imagine my husband wouldn't come home. Sure, I knew women who lost their spouses in action, but I never thought I'd be in the same shoes.

Naïve, I know.

Looking back, I realize I was a complete moron. Mitchell was bigger than life, and he always seemed invincible.

"Maybe you need to go out for an evening and unwind. All this stress isn't good for you." She takes a sip, eyeing me over the rim.

"You're probably right."

"I know Angelo could use a night out too."

I love this woman. She doesn't leave much to the imagination. She doesn't just drop hints, she hurls bombs.

"I'm sure it's not easy for him with the kids."

I know she wants me to take the bait, but I don't. An evening out with Angelo would in no way be a hardship. The man is handsome, sweet, and just one look at him and my body's about to do the horizontal mambo.

She waves me off. "I'll watch the kids. They'll only be little for a short time. I spoil them while I can. You two should go out and get to know each other better." She smirks.

I lean forward and set my mug on the gray and white marble table. "Can I be frank, Betty?"

She nods.

"I don't think Angelo's ready, and I'm not sure I'm the right one for him."

She stares at me for a moment and doesn't speak. I'm truly flattered she wants us to spend time together. What girl wouldn't be when a hot guy's mom thinks you should get to know her son better?

"The one thing I know is my children. Angelo feels things deeper than most people. Losing Marissa almost broke him. But I also know he's not meant to be alone."

"I..."

"I think you two would be perfect for each other."

"Betty," I say, thinking about how to put into words what I feel. "I understand his grief probably better than most people in the world. There's a helplessness and infiniteness to the pain and darkness. It took me a long time before I felt human again. I've never experienced such crushing grief. I know your family wants what's best for him and for him to move on, but until he's ready, there's nothing that will open his heart, not even if he finds the perfect person."

"He's lonely. Even with the kids, he's lonely. I don't think he can escape the darkness until he finds someone with light. Someone who will remind him what it means to be loved and to be a man," she tells me and reaches across the table, touching my hand. "I'm not asking you to love him, dear, but maybe be his friend. As you said, no one else understands what he's going through like you do. Maybe he'll feel comfortable and open up to you. If nothing else, maybe you can help him see there's still more life to live."

I get what she's saying. For years, I avoided going to support groups. I didn't think they'd help. Talking to strangers about something so personal wasn't easy either. But opening up to people, knowing I wasn't alone in how I felt did bring peace, even if only for a little while.

"We could always use more friends. I just don't want you to think that he and I will be anything more."

It almost pains me to say those words. Angelo's a man I could easily fall head over heels for. He's a little intense, but Mitchell wasn't a walk in the park either. Strong men are always a little over the top, and I've never been one to go for the hipster type who wears skinny jeans and spouts sweet words. I need a man with a little bite to him.

Betty nods as she takes another sip of her cocoa. She's stunningly beautiful with her bright red hair and pale skin. "Sure, dear. Of course. If there's no spark, there's no spark."

"Betty." She's goading me, and I'm falling right into her trap. "I never said there wasn't a spark. At least, for me. I just can't rush his heart's ability to move on."

She beams with excitement. "Sure. Sure. I completely understand. Friendship is a great place to start." She dabs the corners of her mouth with her fingertips. "You said you were having some problems getting work done?"

I nod and push away the mug of cocoa. "I am. I have a few things that need doing, and I don't have the skill set to do them." I shrug. "I'll have to look on Craigslist and see who I can find in a pinch."

"Absolutely not." She shakes her head. "I have two men next door who can handle the work. Three, if you include Vinnie who should be home any day now for a few days before his spring break ends."

"I couldn't."

"Doll, let my boys help. They love feeling needed, and right now, you're in need. That's what we do in this neighborhood. We're a small little family, bound not by blood but by location."

I have a feeling that isn't always the case. If I were some crotchety old man with a problem, I wouldn't have three strapping men helping after their momma sent them over to come to my rescue.

"How are your boys going to feel about you offering their services?"

"They'll do whatever I tell them," she says with a smirk.

I have no doubt Betty rules that household. It's the Italian way. I don't think I know any Italian man who isn't wrapped around his mother's finger. There're worse things to be. A man who will adore his mother most likely knows how to treat a woman and has learned respect. That's a way of life I could get behind.

"Let me see if I can find someone else first. If I can't, I'll ask the guys to give me a hand."

She nods again and slides out of the booth. "That's fine."

I rise to my feet, towering over her in my high heels. "Thanks for stopping by," I say, not sure if I should hug her, so I just stand there.

All doubt is wiped away as Betty puts her arms around me and embraces me so tightly, I almost break down in tears. It's been so long since anyone's held me besides Roger. The sentiment is touching, and I know in this moment, not only could I fall for Angelo, but his family too.

CHAPTER EIGHT

ANGELO

TATE HAS her face pressed up against the glass of the cupcake shop. "Where's Tilly?" Tate glances at me before peering through the window again.

"Maybe she's not in yet. Let's go, Tate. Grandma's waiting, and I have work to do."

"Maybe she'll bring me more cupcakes today." Tate runs to my side and grabs my hand. "They were so good, Daddy. Weren't they?" She gazes up at me, wanting nothing more than my attention.

"They were delicious, kiddo. Thanks for sharing with me and Brax."

She smiles. She's proud of herself. The greedy little thing only gave me half of one cupcake, but it was a start. She's never been one to share food, especially dessert. She'd sooner stab you in the hand with her fork than give anyone a bite. She did give Brax an entire cupcake, so I'll take that as a sign of progress.

"Think Tilly can come over sometime?" she asks, totally throwing me for a loop.

I look down at her, and she's gazing up at me with so much hopefulness in her blue eyes. "Maybe, Tate. Tilly's a very busy lady."

"Maybe have her over for dinner. Everyone has to eat," she says like she's thirty years old instead of seven.

"We'll see," I tell her because the last thing I want to do is kill all her joy at eleven in the morning.

She still hasn't forgotten about the horse, something I may never forgive Daphne for mentioning in front of her.

"It would make me so, so happy," she says as we walk through the front door of Hook & Hustle.

The kid has me wrapped around her little finger. She knows it. I know it. Hell, the whole world knows I'm hers to command. Every little girl has her father right where she wants him, and Tate's no exception.

"Grandma!" Tate takes off across the bar, running straight into my mother's waiting arms.

"Hey, kiddo. Ready for a fun day?" Ma lifts her off the floor in the biggest bear hug.

I carry Brax around to the back of the bar with me and set him on top, letting him play with his Transformer for a few more minutes. His tiny feet dangle, kicking the wooden cabinet underneath. "You want something to drink, Brax?"

"No." He doesn't even look at me. He's too fixated on the toy in his hand.

"I want to go ice-skating at the park today," Tate tells my ma, filled with so much excitement at the thought, she's almost shaking.

Lucio walks through the front door and shivers. "Damn, it's cold out there. I'm so sick of this weather."

We're all over the long winter. There have been moments when I thought about joining the other half of my family in Florida, but I can't bring myself to leave my parents behind.

"Don't take off your coat," Ma says to Lucio and then turns to me. "I have something I need both of you to do for a bit today."

She's up to something.

"Who's going to watch the bar?" I ask.

"Your father and I will." She tilts her head, slowly crossing her arms. "I ran this bar more years than you two have. I think we can handle it."

"What on God's green earth do you want us to do?" Lucio asks as he rubs his hands together, trying to warm up.

Ma pitches her head to the side. "Tilly needs help at the shop."

"Wait." Lucio tilts his head. "She needs what kind of help?"

"Her contractor went MIA. She needs a hand

finishing a few projects so she isn't late for the grand opening next week."

"I'll do it." There's no way I'm leaving my parents in charge of the bar, and I sure as shit don't need Lucio to help me give Tilly a hand. "Lucio can stay here."

"I'll help, man," Lucio says immediately.

"No. It's a one-man job."

My mother's smiling for some odd reason. "That's fine too."

Lucio shrugs. "I'll be here if you need me," he tells me before taking off his jacket.

I place Brax back on the floor, guiding him toward his grandma. "Be good today. Listen to Grandma," I tell him and Tate.

Tate gives me a little nod. "We always are, Daddy."

Ma walks over to me and places her hand on my arm. "Thank you," she says. "I have a good feeling about this girl, and I hate to see her struggle. She's been through enough."

"I'll take care of her, Ma."

"You're a good man, baby." She touches my cheek. "Are you sure you don't want Lucio's help?"

I shake my head. "I got it."

Normally, I'd be more than happy to have Lucio's help, but in all honesty, I'm being greedy. I want time with Tilly by myself. The more people around, the more awkward the entire thing could be.

I'd be lying if I didn't admit there's a spark between us. Maybe it's our pasts that draws our souls together.

Unless you've lived through that kind of loss, you can never fully understand the depth of the possible heartache.

"Take your time," Ma says to me. "I'll watch the kids as long as you need. Tilly's waiting for you."

I know what she's doing. I can see her scheme from a mile away. "I won't be too long." I kiss her cheek softly. "Thanks."

I'm thanking her for watching the kids, but I know she already has her eyes set on a possible love affair and future Mrs. Angelo Gallo. She did this with Lucio, pushing him toward Delilah. Of course, he would've found his way to her in time, but Ma and I helped make him come to his senses a little quicker than he would have.

When I walk out of the bar, I stop on the sidewalk between the two buildings and take a few deep breaths. Tilly knocks me off-kilter. Maybe it's the sweet way she talks or the fact that she smells like dessert.

I walk into the cupcake shop, pushing open the front door a little harder than I meant to. I didn't even see the ladder or Tilly standing at the top, polishing a light fixture, until she screeches in horror and tries to grab on to something. She fails, falling backward, and I catch her.

"Jesus, I'm so sorry." I hold her tightly, loving the way she feels in my arms.

"Scared the fuck out of me." She gasps for air. "Thank God you caught me or…"

"I'd never let you fall." I stare into her beautiful green eyes.

She's shaking. "Nothing like almost breaking your neck to remind you of how alive you really are," she says, trying to play off the fact that I could've actually killed her.

I take in her body, light and soft against mine. "What the hell were you doing up that high in heels?"

"I always wear heels." She gives me an innocent smile.

"Always?" I raise an eyebrow, a bit more playful than I normally am.

"Always."

I can imagine her naked in nothing but a pair of red stilettos, standing at the foot of my bed. My stomach flips, liking the idea just as much as my cock does. "I should probably put you down now," I say, but in this moment, I don't really want to. "Ma said you needed help."

"You don't have to. I can hire someone online."

"No. I would love to help."

Her eyes light up. "You would?"

"Don't be silly. I'm ready, willing, and able. I'm here to do whatever you need."

A playful smile dances on her lips. "Well, I guess you better put me down, or we'll get nothing done."

I'd almost forgotten I was still holding her. "Right," I mumble, feeling like a tool. "What do you want me to do first?"

She slides down my body as I release her, a little too close not to be flirtatious. "Well, why don't I show you everything I have on my list, and we'll go from there?"

"I'm your man," I say and stop myself from continuing.

Where the hell did that come from? Again, when I'm around Tilly, I don't feel like Angelo the widower. I feel like Angelo the red-blooded American male.

SIX HOURS LATER, we have the majority of her list completed. Her contractor was ripping her off and working at a snail's pace to get more money out of her. There's no reason any of this shouldn't have been finished already. But in a way, I'm thankful. Without his fuck-up, I wouldn't be sitting next to her on the floor, exhausted and feeling more content than I have in a long time.

"Tilly." I lean against the wall with my arms propped up on my knees. "Want to go to dinner with me? As friends, of course."

I threw in the last little part so I wouldn't scare her off, and it makes me feel less guilty.

"Only if I can pay as a thank you."

I turn my head to face her and narrow my eyes. "Absolutely not. I'm asking you, and therefore, I'm paying. I never let a woman pay."

Her eyebrows rise. "Is this a date?"

I rub the back of my neck, wondering what the hell I'm doing. "I don't know."

Am I taking her out as friends, or do I want something more? I'm not sure where my head or heart is, but it's not in sync with my dick, which very much wants a date with Tilly.

"If we're going out as friends, I can't allow you to pay."

"I'm asking you to dinner. Whatever you want to call it. We barely know anything about each other, but I want to know more about you. I'd like to just kick back, have some food and good company instead of listening to two kids bicker through an entire meal."

She laughs. "Your kids are great, Angelo."

"I wish I could take credit for them being amazing little people, but I think that has more to do with their mother than me."

"Don't sell yourself short. You're amazing with them."

I realize that I just referred to Marissa as their mother instead of my wife for the first time since she died. It feels almost dirty.

"Whatever we're calling it, I'm free tonight," she says, not giving me any more time to dwell on the guilt that has already started to creep in. "Unless that's too soon."

"Tonight would be great," I say quickly because if I put it off, I'll probably chicken out. "It'll be nice."

"Want me to come back here?"

"I'll pick you up." I want to do this thing right.

She stares at me for a moment, biting her lip. "I live in the South Loop. Are you sure it's not too far?"

"Just be ready at eight. I better get back and get the kids."

We both climb to our feet, and there's an awkward moment where we stare at each other.

"I owe you big time for your help, Angelo. I'll make it up to you somehow."

"I didn't do you a favor to have you in my debt. Dinner is payment enough."

For a second, I think she's going to hug me, but she backs away instead. Maybe she feels what I do. An intense connection that's there and undeniable, but there are so many complications in our past, it stops us from acting.

We're in a constant state of immobility.

Trapped by the memories of someone who's no longer here.

CHAPTER NINE

TILLY

ROGER'S SITTING on my bed, typing frantically on his phone as I go through every item of clothing in my closet. "Stop worrying so much."

That's easy for him to say. He's a serial dater, and everything in his closet is spot-on.

"You're not helping." I push all the dresses to one side of the closet and realize everything I own is dressy.

"Wear the black dress."

"Which one?" I own ten black dresses because a girl can never have too many.

"The tight sweater dress with the sweetheart neckline."

"But that's…"

He cuts me off. "It's slutty yet sexy. Not too over the top. The girls will be visible but not on full display. If the man's ready to move on, that number will do the trick."

I lift the dress he's talking about off the rack and stare at it. "It's not really cold-weather friendly, Roger."

"Stop being so practical all the time, Til. Wear a warm coat, and you'll be fine. It's not like you're walking to the restaurant." He laughs, finally tossing his phone to the side when I step out of the closet holding the dress in my hand. "Where are you going anyway?"

"I don't know. He didn't say." I hold the dress against my body and stare at Roger, looking for more of his help. "Hair up or down?"

I usually don't need his input when getting dressed, but I haven't been out with a man in so long, I'm not sure exactly what to do. I feel like a teenager getting ready for a first date without a single fucking clue in life.

"Up. Your neckline is too beautiful to hide, and it'll show off your rack better."

"Roger, if I didn't know better, I'd think you're fond of my breasts."

Roger stands, taking the sweater dress from my hands and grabbing my black push-up bra from the back of my door. "I can still appreciate the female body even if it's not my cup of tea. Wear this and the red stilettos. You'll be a knockout, kid."

I frown, imagining myself all dressed-up and way overdone. "It's not too much?"

"You can never overdress, Til." Roger grabs my shoulders and stares at me. "You like this guy?"

"I think so."

"Stop lying. You wouldn't be going through all this agony over an outfit if you didn't feel something for him."

"Fine," I groan. "I like him."

"Go shower. Shave your legs."

I gawk at him with my mouth hanging open.

"It's best to be prepared. You never know where the night's going to take you."

I shake my head. "I'm not ready for that step."

"Your armor is hairy legs?"

I stick my leg out, running my fingers across the light stubble. "They're not hairy."

"They're not smooth either. Shave them. Leave everything else if you need a safeguard for keeping your newfound virginity."

"Fine." I snatch my dress and bra from his hands.

"If it gets hot and heavy, you may regret your decision."

"Men have it so fucking easy," I mumble.

"Hey. We manscape," Roger says before I close the door to the bathroom.

"Manscape. That's laughable."

I stare at myself in the mirror, wondering how far I'd be willing to go with Angelo if I had the chance. No one has touched me in so long. Today, when I fell and he caught me, I didn't do much to get out of his arms. It felt way too good to have a pair of strong arms surrounding me. I'd almost forgotten how comforting that can be.

Thirty minutes later, I emerge from the bathroom with my hair pulled into a tight bun and the black sweater dress showing off my girls thanks to the help of the push-up bra I typically save for special occasions.

Roger sits up a little straighter on my bed and places his phone in his lap. He whistles. "If there's any hope for this man, he'll be on you like white on rice."

"You're ridiculous." I wave Roger off.

"If I were straight, I'd be all over you."

"That wouldn't be awkward or anything." I snort. "Red lipstick or clear lip gloss?" I hold up two tubes.

Even the smallest decision is giving me trouble. Red lipstick is usually my go-to, but with Angelo, I don't want to come off as a sex kitten looking to get laid. I want the classic beauty without the whorish undertones. I figure the dress already has me halfway to the hooker finish line, and the last thing I want to do is bust through the red tape right onto easy street.

"Red lips are always a must on occasions like this."

"It's a dinner as friends," I remind him, even though I'm dressed like I'm ready to pounce on my prey and get busy.

"I'm sure it's easier for you both to lie to yourselves with that line."

I wonder if that's what we're doing, but there's no time to dissect whatever that is this evening.

As soon as there's a knock at the door, my stomach knots. Maybe this wasn't a good idea. Maybe I'm not ready. No amount of coaching or convincing myself that I am can make it so.

Breathe, Tilly. Breathe.

"It's time." Roger rolls off the bed, looking just as good as he did when he got here. That's the thing about men. They always look the same, and I hate them a little bit for it too. "Too late to back out. Do you want me to call you in a few hours as an out?"

I shake my head, but the option is tempting. "I have to grow up someday, and I don't think I need an exit strategy with Angelo."

Roger grabs my shoulders and squeezes as he stares me in the eyes. "You can do this, Tilly. You deserve this. Allow yourself to enjoy tonight. You're still here and alive, but now you need to start acting on it. Regret's a bitch to live with."

I've had enough regret to last a lifetime. The last thing I need is more. I need to start taking control of my life and allow myself to indulge in things I've abstained from for years.

"Stay in here. I don't want Angelo to get the wrong idea. Let yourself out."

Roger nods. "Have fun. I expect a full rundown tomorrow."

"I wouldn't have it any other way." I give him two quick kisses on each cheek. "Wish me luck."

"You don't need luck with tits like those, Til."

"Coming!" I yell as I run toward the door, leaving Roger in my bedroom, and Angelo knocks again.

I take a deep breath as I touch the doorknob, giving myself a minute to get my shit together. "You got this," I say because somehow saying it out loud makes me feel better. Mental? Maybe, but it works. "It's not a date. We're just friends."

When I open the door, Angelo's leaning against the wall in a white dress shirt, black slacks, and looking yummier than he does when he's wearing a black T-shirt and jeans. The man could wear a paper sack and make it look good.

"Hey." My stomach flutters, and I drink him in.

His eyes travel up my body, and there's a hunger in his eyes. "You're stunning."

My body warms at the compliment, and parts of me that haven't been touched by another human in years remind me they're still alive too.

"Thank you." I stop myself from downplaying the outfit or how I look in it. "You're looking quite dashing yourself."

Dashing isn't the right word. I'm totally out of sync with the realities of dating in my thirties. Who the fuck says dashing anymore?

The man looks straight-up edible. Like I could spend hours exploring every dip and ridge if I were ready for that. I'm big at talking—hell, even thinking about all the naughty things I could do with him.

But would I?

I haven't let another man touch me in so long, I'm not sure I could actually go through with it. My head knows Mitchell isn't here anymore, but my heart hasn't quite caught up.

"Are you ready to go?"

"Yes," I say simply because I don't want to seem overeager about this evening.

I'm excited to be going out with someone, even if we're only friends, because in a city of millions of people, I have very few I consider friends. There's always room for one more, especially a sexy drink of water like Angelo.

He steps to the side, giving me room to pass like a true gentleman. I can feel the heat of his gaze on my back as I walk in front of him. "Where are we going?"

"I thought we'd go for some steak. There's a popular place not too far from here. Unless you'd like something else. But if you're in the mood for something more casual, we can do that too. I'm easy. I like everything."

"I'm kind of in the mood for pizza."

His heavy footsteps stop behind me. "Pizza?"

I glance over my shoulder. "It's my favorite. I heard there's a great place on the South Side, Vito & Nick's."

Angelo's eyebrows rise. "You really want to go to Vito & Nick's?" he asks as he starts walking again to catch up with me.

I nod because there's nothing better than a thin crust pizza covered with hot, gooey cheese and a cold beer to wash it down. "Yeah. Why's that so hard to believe?"

"You just don't look like the pizza type, and then there's your outfit."

I laugh. "I'm very much a pizza girl."

I can feel his body heat against my skin in the cold hallway. "Are you sure?"

I glance upward, taking in his ice-blue eyes and knowing I could get lost in them. "I'm sure. I want to relax, and there's nothing relaxing about a stuffy, over-priced steakhouse."

We're within steps of my building's front door when Angelo places his hand on the small of my back. It's gentle but unmistakable. I'm rendered speechless, almost unable to breathe.

I've missed being touched like this. The move isn't forward or sexual, but manly and comforting. Something Mitchell did often, and I forgot how much I missed so simple an action.

"Pizza, it is." He ushers me outside with his hand still on me. "Whatever makes you happy."

My insides are a jumbled mess. My stomach's fluttering like a horde of butterflies was let loose in a tiny box, banging against the sides and trying to escape.

This man did that to me.

He makes me want and crave things I haven't wanted in far too long.

CHAPTER TEN

ANGELO

THE EVENING'S going better than I ever could've imagined. I haven't felt this comfortable around someone in so long. There hasn't been a moment of quiet, and for that, I'm thankful.

"Another?" I ask, holding the pitcher of beer in my grip as I fill my glass.

Tilly nods and pushes her glass toward me. "I could drink you under the table," she teases and leans over the table. "Don't forget, I grew up on moonshine."

"I beg to differ. I don't drink often with the kids around, but I've been known to hold my liquor better than most."

"Want to put your money where your mouth is?" She raises an eyebrow, challenging me.

God, I love a woman who's willing to gamble, especially on trivial shit that really doesn't matter.

"Maybe. I don't recover as quickly as I used to when I was younger. A hangover with two little kids is *not* fun."

She winces. "I can't even imagine. I don't know how you do it."

"What? Take care of the kids?"

"How you survived," she tells me as her mood darkens, and she stares down at her beer. "I couldn't even take care of myself for a long time. I don't know if I could've kept two kids alive in my grief."

"My family helped for a while, especially Lucio. But you kind of go on autopilot and just take it day by day. There's so much I don't remember from the first year because I went through the motions in a complete fog."

Sometimes I'm surprised we all survived Marissa's death. I couldn't have made it through that dark time without my family. There are days, even now, I'm not sure I can do it, but the kids pull me forward and keep me in the present.

"I know the feeling." She sighs and brings her green eyes back to mine. "Do you ever feel guilty?"

"Every day."

"I feel guilty right now," she admits.

"Do you feel like you're cheating?" I ask.

She nods slowly. "There's always a part of me that's thinking about Mitchell, and being here with you, enjoying your company, somehow feels wrong. Like I'm cheating on his memory and our vows."

I know exactly what she's talking about. Everything feels like a betrayal. Even breathing, when Marissa no longer can, feels wrong. The guilt has waned over time, but sometimes it's still suffocating.

I reach across the table and place my hand on top of hers. "I feel the same way, Tilly. I don't think you can truly love a person and lose them without feeling that way."

"I haven't been out with another man since." She's staring at my fingers as I swipe my thumb across her wrist. "I haven't let another man touch me since then either."

"When you say forever, it's hard to open yourself up again. My family keeps telling me it's time, but…"

"No one knows unless they've been through what we've been through, Angelo."

"This is the closest thing to a date I've done since Marissa died."

I know what you're thinking. What about Michelle, Angelo? Those weren't dates. That wasn't love. There were no feelings involved. We never went all the way either, and I never kissed her on the mouth. It never felt right. That's why I knew there wasn't a future for us, but I wasn't sure how to tell her until she chose to leave town.

In the end, the limited pleasure wasn't worth the guilt I felt afterward.

"Well." Tilly turns her hand over, intertwining her fingers with mine. "Why don't we call this a date, even though it's not. Then we don't have to say we haven't? We'll make this the first part in our comeback, or at least, get a few people off our backs."

"That could work."

A small part of me wishes we were really on a date.

I like Tilly.

I like her a lot.

She's easy, light, and so full of bubbly energy, I want to surround myself with her and never let go.

I hadn't realized I was still holding her hand. It seemed like the most natural thing in the world. We hadn't taken our eyes off each other as our bodies were connected, sitting across the table from each other. This was, in fact, the closest thing I'd had to a date in years.

"Roger says I need to move on and stop living my life in the past."

"He sounds a lot like Daphne and my mother."

"He means well. They all do. I have to be honest with you." She glances down. "Your mother has talked to me about you."

My body tenses, and I don't know how I feel about that. It's everything I'd expect of her. She has balls of steel and isn't afraid to speak her mind. "I'm sorry." It's the only thing I can say. I hate that Tilly felt put on the spot.

"Don't be." She peers up, looking me straight in the eyes. "That's not the part I wanted to be honest about."

"Oh." My eyebrows rise.

"The day we met, with the mixer on the floor, I know I came on really strong, or you could say, a bit crazy."

"It was adorable."

She blushes. "I had made a vow to Roger that I wouldn't be so closed off with the next man who turned my head."

I swallow hard, knowing I was that guy. The one who turned her head.

"I hadn't found any man interesting or truly attractive until you walked into my kitchen with your big muscles and handsome face. You were the first man who made me feel like I wanted more. Like I was ready to move on with my life."

"Really?" I ask, taken aback but also intrigued.

"Yes." She bites her lip. "I feel like a fool telling you this, but in the name of transparency, I want to be honest with you."

I run my finger across the underside of her wrist. "To be honest, I haven't had another woman spark my interest as much as you have in the last few days. You're charming, beautiful, and a little bit of a firecracker. So, in the name of transparency, as you say, I like you a lot, and I'm not entirely sure how I feel about that."

Tilly beams. "I'm okay with that."

"Me too." My heart's racing, so I'd say a part of me

is more alive than I have been in years. "I think we should be friends, and if something more comes of it, so be it. We can't rush these things, especially with our history, no matter how badly our friends and family want us to."

"So, is this officially a date?" She looks at me with so much hope in her eyes.

"Yes," I tell her because, for the first time in forever, I can say the words without the knot forming in my stomach. "It's a date."

"Pepperoni well done," the waitress says as she stands beside our table with the pie in her hand.

I don't look up or pull away.

I don't want to.

"Oh, sorry." Tilly slides her hand back, breaking our contact. "Smell that," she says as the waitress sets the pizza in the middle of the table. "That's what you call heaven."

While I love my pizza, I could think of so many other things that would top my list of heavenly smells. Tilly's scent would be one of them. Marissa always wore Chanel No 5, but Tilly smells like the sweetest confection.

"I would've thought cupcakes were your favorite food."

She shakes her head as she pulls the first slice onto her plate. "Nope. I love them, but I'm all about the pizza."

I like a chick who can wear five-inch heels, a little

black dress that leaves little to the imagination, and downs cheap beer and piping hot slices of pepperoni.

"You're different than I expected." I watch as she takes a giant bite without giving two shits about burning her mouth.

She opens her mouth, waving her hand frantically in front of her face. "Oh fuck." Tears start to form in her eyes, and she grabs her beer, chugging half the glass.

"Are you okay?"

"Who needs all that skin on the roof of your mouth anyway? Hell, taste buds are overrated too." She laughs, wiping the tears from her eyes.

I push my glass of ice water across the table. "Drink," I tell her.

She doesn't hesitate in taking the glass and downing the entire thing in a few gulps. "Christ. Okay. Maybe it's not that bad." She laughs again.

"Do you want to go?"

"No. I'm going to make this pizza pay for burning my mouth."

It's my turn to laugh. She has the best attitude about everything. I can't imagine her being down a day in her life. Knowing what she went through, losing her husband, I know there's still hope for me.

"Don't hold back on my account. I love a woman who can eat."

"Well, Ang, you're about to see me demolish the hell out of this bad boy." She takes a smaller bite this time, careful not to have a repeat performance. "Eat fast or risk starvation," she tells me.

I only take a few slices, putting them on my plate for safekeeping. I really want to see how much this little redhead can put away. She's great at shit-talking, but I need to know if she can back it up. I'm giving her free rein over the remaining two-thirds of the pizza.

"Do your damage," I tell her, loving the little noises she makes with each bite.

My cock seems to like it too. Each moan causes the fucker to twitch, telling me I better get my shit together. Three years is a long time to go without being inside a woman, vows or no vows. I said the words, not my cock and balls, and they're starting to revolt.

I'm slow to eat my pizza, staring at Tilly in amazement as she puts away each slice like she's an NFL linebacker and not a Southern lady who wouldn't be caught dead in a pair of blue jeans. In under thirty minutes, she polishes off every slice of pizza on the tray and half a pitcher of beer.

"I'm stuffed." She dabs her lips with the napkin.

I stare at her in amazement and shake my head. "I don't know where you put it."

She drops the napkin to the plate and grips her stomach. "You can't lay down a challenge and not expect me to follow through. I'm as competitive as they come."

"I can see that." I can't wipe the dopey smile off my face. "You want more to drink?"

She shakes her head. "I seriously can't fit another

thing inside me, or I'll look more like a sausage roll in this dress than an actual human."

"Don't be silly. You're a knockout."

"It's been a long time since a man has flirted with me." She touches the base of her throat, drawing my eyes away from her face. "I could get used to this."

"I highly doubt I'm the first. Maybe you just weren't listening. If a man has a pulse, he's at least thinking what I'm saying."

She blushes again. "I'm sure all the ladies are after you."

I shake my head and laugh. "A single father isn't really most-eligible-bachelor material."

"A handsome man with two children whom he loves and cherishes is most definitely a head-turner."

"Well, my attitude sometimes has a way of putting women off."

"You're intense, but that shows you're passionate."

"I'll remember that the next time my sister tells me to stop being an asshole. I'll just tell her I'm passionate."

Tilly laughs loudly. "That one may not go over so well."

"She'll probably smack me," I say, laughing with her.

Tilly sobers. "She loves you, though. You don't know how lucky you are to have three siblings. I have no one except me."

"I can't imagine. I'm sorry."

The thought of being an only child is so foreign to me. Yeah, the house would've been quieter growing up, but there would've been so much boredom in the silence.

She waves me off. "Don't be sorry. I don't really know what it's like to have a brother or sister."

"Loud."

She laughs again. "I could get used to a little noise."

"Roger seems to care about you," I tell her, prying into their relationship.

He didn't seem to be happy when he found me in the kitchen at her shop. Roger was overprotective, almost like he was sweet on her.

She sighs. "When his brother died, he made it his mission to make sure I was okay. He cares too much sometimes, but he's not in love with me, if that's what you're hinting at."

"I wasn't."

But I was.

No man sticks around that long and is that fierce about someone unless they love them.

She smirks, probably not buying my statement. "Mitchell was his only sibling. I guess Roger adopted me in a way so he wouldn't be as lonely too. Besides—" she leans forward with her chin resting against her fingers "—he'd more likely be into you than me."

"Oh." I laugh, feeling like a complete tool for thinking I was going to have to worry about Roger.

"Yeah. He's a good guy, though."

"You want to get out of here?"

"I'm sure you need to get home to the kids."

"They're sleeping by now. I don't live too far from here. Maybe we can swing by and check on them before we head back downtown."

"I'd love that," she says and grabs her purse off the table, standing as I do.

While I do want to check on the kids, I really want to be alone with Tilly. I'd like nothing more than to kick up our feet and talk until the wee hours of the morning instead of sitting in a pizza shop on the far South Side. I'm not ready for the evening to be over. Not quite yet.

She walks in front of me as we walk outside. The wind kicks up, and her vanilla scent surrounds me. There's a peacefulness to the smell. Comfort. I place my hand on the small of her back, guiding her toward my car.

"Are you sure it's okay?" I ask because the last thing I want to do is make her feel uncomfortable.

She turns her face toward me. "Your hand or your house?"

"Both."

"They're more than okay, Angelo."

In this moment, standing in the parking lot and touching her, it's the first time I've wanted to kiss someone other than my wife.

CHAPTER ELEVEN

TILLY

Angelo was just going to run in and check on the kids, but I asked him if I could come in, being more forward than I ever have been.

I wasn't ready to call it a night. Spending time with him was no hardship. He made me feel good about myself and more like the old me. The one before Mitchell died.

His house is charming and warm. Everything I'd expect inside a house filled with little kids. Toys are everywhere. But walking across wood floors covered in Legos isn't easy in five-inch heels. I sit on the edge of the couch, watching him as he pays the babysitter before she rushes out of the house.

"You're really okay with this?" Angelo asks as he sits next to me.

"How could I not be? This is perfect." I ease back into the most comfortable couch I've ever sat on. "I'll grab a taxi later. That's the best part of living in the city."

"At least the kids are asleep. Take off your shoes and put your feet up. Relax a little." Angelo stares at my feet and grimaces. "I don't know how you wear those things."

I pry the leather shoes from my feet and drop them between the table and the couch. "I'm ridiculously short without them."

Even with me wearing the heels, Angelo towers over me. Most people do. The extra height makes me more confident. They're like my battle armor. I feel invincible as soon as I gain a few inches. It's weird. I know. But you'd have to walk a mile with my short-ass legs to understand.

"How short?" He raises one eyebrow.

"I probably wouldn't even come up to your chin." I giggle.

He stands and holds out his hands, wiggling his fingers. "Let me see."

I slide my fingers across his, gripping his hands tightly. I almost squeal when he pulls me to my feet like I weigh nothing. The power in his arms is so freaking hot, but somehow, I maintain my dignity. "See." I peer up at him as we stand only a few inches apart.

He tightens his grip, and the air shifts. "I like you shorter."

My stomach flips. "Well, I…" I go suddenly stupid because the man's looking at me like I'm one of those cupcakes I have in my display. "I feel so small compared to you."

Angelo's not only tall, he's built like a beast. Wide shoulders and bulging muscles everywhere. "You are." He tucks a strand of hair behind my ear that has fallen free from my updo.

The gesture's so sweet, I practically melt into a pile of goo right before his eyes. When his fingers slide down and he cups my face in his hand, I damn near lose it.

"Do you feel that?" he asks in a sexy, deep voice that would make any lady weak in the knees.

"Yeah," I whisper, unable to take my eyes off his.

He doesn't have to explain what he's talking about. I feel everything, and there's no denying the attraction. Maybe our souls are drawn to each other. Kindred spirits bound by our grief, and they can only find reprieve and comfort in the other. Kismet built of misery.

We stare at each other with one hand still locked together and his other hand still on my face. My skin breaks out in goose bumps, loving the feel of his thumb grazing my cheek.

I want to kiss him so badly. More than I've wanted to kiss someone in years. My body craves his touch.

"I want to kiss you," he says like he's unsure and maybe asking permission.

"I want you to kiss me too."

He leans forward, gazing at me with nothing short of pure fire. His eyes search my face, and I feel the full heat of his stare. He moves his hand, releasing his grip on my fingers, and slides it around my back. There's a moment that passes between us as our breathing picks up and I swear I can hear the pounding of his heart. It matches my own.

The closer he gets, the faster my heart beats. It's been so long since I've kissed anyone on the lips. I almost wonder if I even know how to kiss properly anymore or if I'll fail miserably. All the doubt I felt as an awkward teenager comes rushing back, and my body shakes.

"Are you okay?" he asks with his lips only inches from mine.

"Do it," I reply, unable to take my eyes off him. "Kiss me."

I need his lips against mine more than I need the air in my lungs. The past doesn't exist. The future is unknown. All we have is this moment. This kiss.

His fingers tighten behind my neck, pulling my face to his. The heat I saw earlier in his eyes has turned into a raging inferno.

I lean into him, waiting for his mouth, and close my eyes. I'm practically begging for the kiss, and my body's vibrating with anticipation. A kiss shouldn't be this monumental, but this one is.

At first, he kisses me so gently, I almost don't feel his lips against mine. My skin tingles, and my heart's beating wildly out of control because I know there's no turning back now. I wouldn't want to either. In five years, no man has even turned my head, but Angelo's not only hot, he understands me.

My front presses against his chest, loving the hardness of him as he wraps one arm around my back and eliminates all the space between us. We stand there, kissing softly, bodies pressed together, and nothing else seems to matter.

Live in the present. I remind myself of the mantra I promised to follow for the last two years. There is nothing more present than Angelo and the way he's holding me in his arms. His smell, spicy and full man, surrounds me and roots me in the moment.

He pulls away and stares down at me. "Do you want to stop?" he whispers.

"No." I slide my hands up his arms and lock my fingers behind his neck. "Kiss me like we only have tonight."

His eyes search mine for a moment, then his mouth is on mine. This time, a little harder than before, but he's still holding back. I slide my fingers up the back of his neck, tethering myself to him and pulling his face closer.

He has me weak in the knees the moment he turns

his head and his teeth tug at my bottom lip. I moan my appreciation, wanting more, needing to taste him. I could stay like this forever. The rest of the world be damned.

I haven't felt this much pure joy and sheer pleasure in five long years. There's nothing like the touch of another person or the lips of a hot man, reminding me I'm alive and there's more than just sadness left in my body.

I want him. I want his kiss. I want his arms. I want everything he has to give.

He walks me backward, easing me onto the couch and covering me with his body. But his hands stay at my sides, careful not to go further. I can appreciate that. I could lose myself in this man, but I'm not sure either of us is ready for more than the way we're kissing each other.

His weight is delicious on top of me. I feel so small underneath his massive frame. Protected and cocooned. My body's on fire, getting ahead of my mind.

Then it happens. Angelo sweeps his tongue inside my mouth, giving me the first taste of his sweetness. My hands roam his back as our tongues tangle together, speaking to each other without saying a word. I dig my fingernails into his shoulders, wanting more—and needing it just as much too.

CHAPTER TWELVE

ANGELO

"Daddy."

I grunt as Tate pulls on my arm.

"Daddy," she whispers and tugs harder.

"Baby, let Daddy sleep." I don't open my eyes.

"Why's Tilly here?" Tate asks.

Every muscle in my body tenses as my eyes fly open.

Fuck.

I'm about to get the Shittiest Father of the Year award. The one thing I promised myself was that I wouldn't subject my kids to someone I was dating until I was pretty damn serious about where our future was heading.

I'm not quite sure where Tilly and I are going. Last night, kissing her made me feel alive again. It made me want more of her. I'd been so busy with the kids and the bar, I'd put the loneliness I felt completely out of my mind.

Everything about us felt right. She got me. She didn't judge me on my sadness or guilt. Tilly had walked in my shoes, losing the person she thought she'd spend eternity with.

"We fell asleep watching a movie, baby." I glance down at Tilly, who's still sleeping peacefully at my side. Thank God shit didn't get out of hand and we are both fully clothed. That would've been a complete nightmare.

This is bad.

Tate's on the coffee table, staring at the two of us. Her tiny legs are kicking back and forth against the wood, and I know she probably has a million questions. She pushes her unruly hair backward and yawns before rubbing the sleep from her eyes. "Are you going to make us breakfast?"

She doesn't seem bothered or even shocked that Tilly's in our home and spent the night, but the guilt in my gut is clear as day. As a father, it's my duty to protect Tate, even if it's from me.

"I don't know. Tilly probably has to go," I tell her.

Tilly starts to stir in the crook of my arm. It's like I'm frozen. I don't know if I should push Tilly away, putting space between us for Tate. But I also don't want to be an asshole to Tilly and have her wake up in the middle of me shoving her off my shoulder.

Tate scrunches her little nose. "Why?"

"Well…"

"Oh my God," Tilly whispers at my side and tenses just like I did.

Tate giggles. "Morning, Tilly."

If the kid's traumatized by Tilly's presence, she's not letting on. Tate seems excited there's another woman in the house, and it doesn't hurt that Tilly's always giving her cupcakes.

"I'm sorry." Tilly pushes herself upright while glancing up at me with nothing but fear in her eyes.

"Don't be sorry," Tate answers for me. "Daddy was just going to make us breakfast."

Tate and her food. She'd probably be more upset about missing a meal than she is about finding Tilly and me fast asleep on the couch.

"I should go." Tilly scoots to the edge of the couch. She's about to get up, but Tate puts her hand out, stopping Tilly in her tracks.

"No." Tate shakes her head. "You can't."

I move to the edge of the couch next to Tilly. "Why not?"

Tate toys with the edge of her unicorn nightgown, looking at us from under her ridiculously long eyelashes. "Because she's hungry."

"I'm not really much of a morning eater," Tilly tells Tate.

Tate's mouth drops open, and she lowers her head. "You don't eat breakfast?"

Tilly looks at me out of the corner of her eye and grimaces. "No."

Tate's still in shock. She's staring at Tilly like she's an oddity in a sideshow. "I'd die of starvation."

I glance at Tilly and roll my eyes. "She's a little dramatic."

Tate crosses her arms and narrows her eyes. "I am not."

"And she's feisty in the morning."

"I'm hungry," she whines and points to her stomach, always ready to eat. "Can you make Tilly and me pancakes?"

I don't even bother arguing with her. There's no getting her to change her mind when her belly isn't full. She's like a little monster. She takes hangry to a whole new level.

"You should stay," I tell Tilly because I want her to know I'm okay with it.

If Tate's not freaking out about Tilly being there, I can let it slide if it makes her happy. Plus, it'll be nice to have an adult to talk to over breakfast instead of just two little kids.

Tate jumps from the coffee table and starts to run around the room, cheering in victory. "Best breakfast ever!" She pumps her fists in the air.

Tilly turns toward me until our knees are almost touching. "Are you sure?"

I remember the way she made me feel last night. "I am. Plus—" I tick my chin toward Tate who's still celebrating her victory "—she's happy, and so am I. I'll start breakfast. You just relax."

I want to kiss her again, but I stop myself. Tate's seen enough for one day, and kissing Tilly in front of her wouldn't be right.

Tate stands near the hallway, waving her arms. "Tilly, come see my room."

She's adorable, even when she's a total pain in my ass. If I'm not careful, my mother and sister will turn her into a monster by the time she's eighteen. The thought alone gives me a headache.

Tilly slides her hands into mine, and I pull her up from the couch. "Go see her room. I've got this handled."

She nods, biting her bottom lip and driving me a little crazy. Morning wood is a real thing, and right now, I'm suffering.

Between last night and the crazy dream I had about Tilly wearing nothing but those hot-as-fuck red stilettos, I knew I was on the verge of blue balls.

Tate grabs Tilly's hand and pulls her toward the hallway. "Come on," she says to her, impatient as always.

I stand there, watching them as they walk hand in hand toward Tate's bedroom.

Part of me is happy to see Tate content and seeming to latch on to Tilly so easily. But there is another part, the one that's become a part of me since Marissa took her last breath, that makes me feel like I am betraying the memory of my wife.

"Daddy," Tate calls out, turning around near her doorway. "We want chocolate chips and bananas in the pancakes."

"Sure, baby." There isn't any reason to argue. The kid isn't giving me any problems about Tilly being here. Chocolate chips and bananas are always her favorite combination.

"You want plain, Tilly?" I ask.

"Chocolate and bananas are perfect."

"There's nothing better, and my daddy makes the best pancakes in the world."

The kid clearly needs to get out more. I am okay at pancakes, but there's not much you can fuck up about pouring some batter and turning it over before charring one side.

Brax wanders out of his room, rubbing his eyes with his tiny fists and doesn't even stop to look in Tate's room, even when he has to hear two voices.

"I'm hungry." He stands in the middle of the kitchen, making my job of prepping the pancakes a little more difficult.

I lift him up, placing his ass on the middle island so he's out of the way and can't get into too much trouble. "You can help," I tell him, but there's no way I'm letting him mix a damn thing.

I place three bananas in a plastic bag, seal it tightly, and hand it off to Brax to smash into tiny pieces. It's enough to keep him occupied while I finish everything else.

"Who's Tate talking to?" He uses all his might to mash the bananas, staring at the plastic bag with so much focus.

"Tilly."

Brax's eyes widen. "Yay!" he says, sounding every bit like his sister. "I like Twilly."

"Daddy, can I wear my pink dress?" Tate yells from her room. "Tilly's going to help me get ready."

I stare down the hallway, caught off guard. I don't answer right away.

"Daddy!"

"Sure," I yell back, but I'm not sure if I've totally fucked everything up.

As I finish prepping breakfast, I analyze all the ways I could've messed up my children by having a woman in the house. Every book I read on grieving and how to move forward with children said to introduce children to new "friends" slowly. The last thing I wanted was for them to get attached to someone who wouldn't be a permanent fixture in my life.

There's a knock on the door, but I'm knee-deep in batter, and the griddle is covered with pancakes. Before I can move, Tate comes running out of her bedroom and heads toward the door. Her hair is tied up in a pink bow, and she's wearing her favorite pink dress.

Tilly walks out behind her and comes my way. "Are you sure this is okay?"

"I am."

"She insisted I help her get ready."

"She's demanding. I'm sorry." I flip the pancakes.

"Vinnie," Tate screams so loudly, my ears ring.

Moments later, Lucio and Vinnie, with Tate in his arms, walk into the kitchen and stop dead in their tracks. They look at Tilly and then to me with their mouths hanging open.

"It's not what it looks like."

"Daddy had a sleepover," Tate tells them, throwing me right under the bus.

"I have a lot of those too." Vinnie has the biggest freaking smirk.

"Hey," I warn because the kid doesn't need to know about the endless stream of women my brother has in his bed.

"We were watching a movie and fell asleep on the couch."

"So." Lucio slides onto a stool on the other side of the island. "You making enough for everyone?"

He's letting the entire Tilly sleepover slide now, but I know as soon as we're alone, he's going to grill me.

"Maybe I better go." Tilly fidgets next to me.

I glance over at her. "Stay."

"Tilly has to stay." Tate grabs Vinnie's face. "She gives me cupcakes."

Vinnie laughs. "A girl after my own heart."

"Vinnie, why don't you and Tate set the table?" I tell

him before he has a chance to say something I know I'll want to slap him for.

"Sure. Want to help me, baby girl?" he asks Tate before blowing a raspberry in the crook of her neck. She squeals and tips her head back, loving every minute of the way my brothers fawn over her.

"How's the shop coming, Tilly? Did Angelo get everything done?" Lucio asks.

"He was a big help." Tilly leans over the end of the counter, keeping a safe distance from me.

"I'm sure he was," Vinnie mumbles and earns the evil eye from me.

"Good." Lucio doesn't say anything more.

"Why's everyone here so early? It's not even nine." I ask while I take the pancakes off the griddle.

"We had to run to the restaurant supply store, and since your place is on the way back, I figured we'd stop and see how you were doing. Vinnie wanted to talk to you too."

"About?" I glance at Vinnie because the only time he wants to see me is when he needs something.

"It can wait. I'll talk to you at the bar," Vinnie says before he turns his attention toward Tilly. "So, Tilly. Why cupcakes?"

"Why not?" she shoots back at him.

I laugh as I check the undersides of the second batch of pancakes, liking the way she isn't a shy little mouse around my brothers.

"Fair enough." Vinnie nods, placing the last plate on the table. "What's the best one you make?"

"My double caramel pecan turtle cupcake. You should stop in and try it. I made a new batch yesterday."

"I'm there," he replies quickly. "It takes a lot of calories to maintain this body."

I roll my eyes because he's flexing, showing off his muscles, which are almost out of control.

"Your head's looking smaller than usual," Lucio tells him, saying exactly what I was thinking. "You get any bigger, and other things may start to shrink as well."

I laugh and glance at Tilly. She's laughing but covering her mouth, trying to hide her amusement.

"You can fluff off, brother," Vinnie snaps.

"Fluff?" Tilly's eyebrows draw inward.

"We try not to swear in front of the kids," Lucio tells her. "We have to be creative."

"Cute," Tilly replies.

I flip the pancake onto the platter, wanting to feed the troops so they can get the fuck out. "Breakfast is done."

"I want to sit next to Tilly and Vinnie," Tate announces. "Is that okay, Daddy?"

"Anything you want, sweetheart." Somehow, I've become her third priority in a room full of people.

Lucio grabs the platter off the counter and nudges me with his elbow. "We have a lot to talk about," he whispers as everyone sits down at the table, waiting to eat.

"We'll talk later," I tell him, knowing he's going to have a lot to say.

"You surprised me this morning." He motions toward Tilly with his chin. "You took a big step."

Hell, I surprised myself. I was reckless with Tilly. Something I'd promised myself I'd never be with my children. Although I haven't said it, I think it's time to backpedal a little, putting my kids before myself. Even if that means keeping whatever Tilly and I have on hold.

CHAPTER THIRTEEN

TILLY

"WELL, WELL, WELL." Roger leans against the building outside the bakery, staring at me as I climb out of my car. "Look what the cat dragged in."

"Don't say it." I stalk past him and barely make eye contact.

"Tilly, I'm not judging you."

He doesn't need to say the words. I know Roger would never judge me, especially after everything he's been through with me the last five years.

My hands are shaking, and putting the key in the lock of the shop's front door is virtually impossible. "Stupid door," I groan.

"Gimme." Roger takes the keys from my hand, easily unlocking the shop. "You're out of sorts today."

"Just today?" I snort. "I've been out of sorts for years."

There's no normal after loss. Last night was the first time I felt anything even remotely like the old me. But this morning, when I woke up on Angelo's couch with Tate staring at us, all my newfound normalcy flew right out the window.

Roger follows me into the shop and shrugs off his jacket, throwing it on a banquette chair near the doorway. "That's not true. You've been doing well for a long time. This last week, I saw a glimpse of the old Tilly."

I spin around on my heels and tap my foot against the marble tile. "And who is the old Tilly?"

He rubs his hands together and tilts his head, probably trying to figure out if I'm about to lose my shit entirely. "The old Tilly is playful and fun. Her smile is infectious and flirtatious." He takes a few steps forward, easily closing the space between us, and grabs my shoulders. "She's happy."

I sigh. "I feel more like myself than I have in years, even today, but…"

"What happened last night? Was he an asshole?" He narrows his eyes, trying to read more into my statement than what I actually said. "Because I'll kick his ass."

I can't stop myself from laughing. Although Roger's built, I don't think he's thrown a punch in ten years, which I'm sure hasn't been the case for Angelo. "You aren't going to hurt Angelo."

"I will if he hurt you."

I wrap my arms around Roger's middle and rest my head on his chest. "Angelo was a perfect gentleman last night, Roger. Don't be overdramatic."

He places his hands on my back, holding me tightly like he's done so many other days. "Then what's wrong?"

"We kissed," I whisper into his dress shirt. "A lot."

"That's great, Til," he says sweetly. "That's a big step for you."

"Can I be honest?"

He moves his head backward and glances down at me. "Always, doll."

"When we were kissing, everything was great. But afterward, when I woke up this morning, I felt like I was cheating on Mitchell."

Roger moves one hand off my back and brings his fingers to my chin, forcing me to look at him. "You can't think that way."

"I do, though."

He has both hands on my face now. "Hey," he whispers when I try to look everywhere else except his eyes. "Look at me."

For a moment, I keep my gaze trained on the cupcake case because this isn't a conversation I am ready to have with Roger. He's been trying to get me to find my happiness for years, but even talking with him about last night seems like a betrayal.

"I'm proud of you," he says softly as soon as I finally look at him.

"For what? Kissing a man?"

"For taking that step. It's a big one."

I fist the sides of his dress shirt, tethering myself to him. "Will I ever get past the point of feeling like I'm cheating on your brother?"

Roger sighs. "There's no one in the world who loved my brother as much as you, Tilly, besides me. Sometimes even I feel guilty."

My eyes widen. "For what?"

"For everything."

"That's silly."

"No. It's not." I can see the pain in his eyes. "Mitchell isn't here, standing with you today with his arms wrapped around you. I'm here in his place instead. There are moments where I'm happy, flying high on life, and then it all comes crashing down around me when I realize my brother won't experience that type of joy again."

Tears form in my eyes. Sometimes, I forget I'm not alone in my grief. Moments like this, when we're being raw and honest, remind me Roger's lost just as much.

"Don't cry." He swipes his thumbs over the top of my cheeks, wiping away my tears. "We've cried enough."

I don't think I'll ever cry enough tears for Mitchell.

There were so many days when I thought I didn't have another tear to shed, only to end up bawling my eyes out because of a song on the radio or a memory of something sweet from the past.

"Now tell me what happened. Maybe I can help you figure out what's really causing you so much pain."

I swallow hard before taking a deep breath, trying to calm myself down. "When we woke up this morning, Tate was staring at us."

Roger's eyes widen. "Oh shit."

"We were dressed. We fell asleep on the couch, but still. I felt so shitty that she found me there."

"Was she upset?"

I shake my head. "She made me help her get dressed and do her hair, and she insisted I stay for breakfast."

Roger smiles sweetly. "It sounds like Tate's quite taken with you."

"But…"

Roger raises an eyebrow. "Tilly, Tate's been through more trauma than finding a fully dressed woman sleeping on her father's couch."

I know he's right. The kid's been through more in her first seven years than I did in my first twenty. But that doesn't make it easier for me to swallow or for any of it to feel right.

"She shouldn't have found me there."

"How did you sleep?"

"The best sleep I've had in years."

I haven't slept well since the day the men showed up

on my doorstep, telling me the news of Mitchell's death. But last night was the first night I slept peacefully.

"I'm sure Angelo's feeling a lot of what you are today, sweetheart. You should talk to him about it."

"I will," I promise him. "You aren't mad at me?"

He looks at me funny. "For what?"

"Kissing Angelo and staying over at his place."

"Tilly, there's nothing you can do to make me mad. If you're alone forever because you can't move on, I'll be pissed. But you can never make me upset by finding your happiness."

The bell above the front door rings. "Tilly," Tate says from behind me.

I turn, moving out of Roger's arms. "Tate, baby. What are you doing here?"

She's eyeing Roger, probably wondering who the man is who's touching me. "Who's that man?"

I walk toward Tate and crouch down so we're eye-to-eye. "This is Roger. He's my brother."

There's no other way to describe him, especially to a seven-year-old. Roger's the only family I have. Even though we're not related by blood, he's mine forever. No two people could go through what we endured and not have an eternal and lasting bond.

"You have a brother like me?" she whispers.

I nod.

Tate steps around me and cranes her neck upward to look at Roger as he approaches. "I'm Tate," she tells him.

Roger laughs. "I'm Roger."

"You're lucky."

"For what?" Roger asks Tate.

She motions for him to bend down, and he does. "Because you have a sister like Tilly," Tate whispers. "And she makes the best cupcakes in the world."

Roger laughs again. It's hard not to with a kid like Tate. "I like this kid."

"She's a hungry little thing." Vinnie pats her on the shoulder. "Just like her uncle. I'm sorry we barged in here like that."

I wave him off. "It's fine, Vinnie. You're always welcome." I turn toward Tate, who's moved her attention toward the display case. "Tate too."

Vinnie rubs the back of his neck. "Tate insisted we come get her daily cupcake."

"Kid forgets nothing," I say with a laugh.

"Not when it comes to food."

"Why don't you help her pick something out and whatever you'd like too."

Vinnie's eyes light up. "Are you sure? I'm happy to pay."

I shake my head. "I insist."

Vinnie nods before joining Tate by the display case. I watch them as they stand hand in hand, staring at all the cupcakes.

"He's a hot one." Roger leans over and whispers in my ear.

"He's like twenty years old."

"They must be descendants of Roman gods. I mean, look at that." He motions toward Vinnie's ass as he bends over to talk to Tate.

I smack his chest with the back of my hand. "You need help."

He shrugs. "I'm going to take out the trash for you, and then I have to run."

"Where are you going so early?"

"I have a meeting at noon with a new client."

"Call me later?" I ask.

He leans forward and kisses my cheek. "You'll be the first to hear how it went. Now go get the kid a cupcake before she slobbers all over the glass."

I smack him again. For all the love Roger has to give, he's not much of a kid person. His apartment and clothes are immaculate, and there's no place for a messy kid in his life. He'd be a great father if he'd let go of some of his obsessive cleaning disorder.

"So." I walk toward Vinnie and Tate as Roger disappears into the back room. "What looks good?"

"Everything," Tate whispers with wide eyes.

"These are really something, Tilly." Vinnie looks up at me over the case. "I can see why she insisted we come here."

"I like seeing her so happy."

Kids are resilient. With everything she's been through, she deserves to have a smile on her face always. A cupcake is the least I can do to make that happen.

"You seem to have that effect on a lot of people in our family," Vinnie says, knocking the wind out of me.

"What's that one called?" Tate points to the cupcake covered in chocolate frosting and bits of dried banana.

"That's the Funky Monkey."

Tate erupts in laughter.

"You want one?"

"Yes!"

"Make it two," Vinnie says. "We'll take them back next door because we've taken up enough of your time."

"You're welcome to stay as long as you want."

Sometimes the quiet in the shop is almost too much for me to bear. I can't wait for the day I officially open the doors and there're people bursting at the seams, allowing me to focus less on who's missing and more on what's ahead.

"Thanks, Tilly," Tate says as I hand her a box with two Funky Monkeys. "You're the best."

She's buttering me up, and I'm swallowing it hook, line, and sinker. Tate's charming, just like the rest of her family. She's someone I have quickly found myself pulled toward, and I could easily love her as my own.

"Stop over for a drink or some food later," Vinnie says. "I'm sure my brother would like to see you."

I nod my head, but I'm not sure about being in Angelo's presence at this moment. I could fall hard for that man, but am I ready to take that step?

"See you later, Tilly." Tate holds her box like it contains a treasure.

I wave, not moving otherwise as I watch them walk out the front door and head next door to the bar. Angelo's entire family is something I've always dreamed about. Growing up as an only child was lonely and sometimes smothering because my parents focused their attention only on me. I wonder what it would've been like to grow up with so many brothers and never have that feeling of being truly alone.

"Roger," I call out when I hear the back door slam shut. I figured he'd come back out front and say goodbye, but he disappeared without another word.

When I walk into the kitchen, I see an envelope propped up next to my mixer with my name written in Mitchell's handwriting. I run, snatching up the paper as quickly as possible, and drag my fingers across the script.

When I turn it over, there's a Post-it from Roger.

Don't open until later. Love, Roger xoxo

CHAPTER FOURTEEN

ANGELO

"Do you love me?" Marissa asks as she gazes up at me. *Her hand's covering my heart, warming my skin from the cool fall breeze.*

"I do." I cover her hand with my own. "More than the stars in the sky above us."

"Will you forget me?"

"How could I?"

She props herself up on her elbow, hovering above me. "You need to move on," she says softly. "I can't stay with you forever."

I slide my hand against her cheek, cupping her face in my palm. "I want to be with you always."

"I'll always be here." She presses softly against my

chest. "Watching over you. But it's time," she tells me as her body starts to fade.

I gasp, sitting straight up, half asleep with tears streaming down my face. My dreams of Marissa have virtually stopped. It's been over a year since I've seen her when I close my eyes. I'm both comforted and over-come with grief from the dream, feeling like I lost her all over again.

I swing my legs over the side of the bed, letting the tears fall to the floor. I feel such anger in this moment, wishing I could crawl back into the dream and hating myself for waking up.

"Come back," I whisper into the darkness. "Just one more time."

She's never said those words to me before. Not in a dream, at least. It's like she was saying goodbye again, ripping my heart into a million little pieces.

"Promise me, Angelo."

The words she begged me to say come back to me, slamming into my chest like a sledgehammer. I would've promised her my celibacy if it meant she'd be happy. That's all I ever wanted—besides her next to me.

The clock on the nightstand ticks over to midnight, and I know there's no way I'm getting back to sleep anytime soon.

I grab my phone and tiptoe down the hallway, careful not to wake the kids. The screen flashes as I pour myself a glass of whiskey, and I collapse onto the couch.

Tilly: I can't sleep. Sorry for the late text, but I was thinking of you.

I stare at the screen and take the first biting sip of whiskey, wondering if Marissa knows about Tilly and is doing something to push us together.

I've been at war with myself since this morning when Tate found us on the couch. Kissing Tilly was the closest thing to happiness I've felt since Marissa last lay in my arms. I spent half the day wondering if I should tell Tilly we needed to slow down, and I still hadn't made a decision when I fell asleep.

I lean back into the couch, placing the whiskey on the table next to me and open Tilly's text message.

"Is this what you want?" I look around the room like Marissa's going to appear before I type out my reply.

Me: I can't sleep either, and it was nice to wake up to your text.

I take another sip, waiting for Tilly's reply, and try to shake off the sadness that's settled in my soul from the dream of Marissa.

Tilly: I barely sleep anymore.

Me: Me either.

Tilly: The only night I've slept well was last night.

Her words hit me square in the chest. When we fell asleep on the couch, I couldn't believe I didn't wake up before Tate. I hadn't slept in later than her in three years. I spent every night tossing and turning, reaching for Marissa, only to find nothing but emptiness.

Me: Me too, actually.

Tilly: Are we moving too fast?

I laugh and shake my head, realizing everything I've been feeling is normal. I'm not alone in my unease, or in finding the ability to move forward almost paralyzing.

Me: I don't know, Tilly. All I know is that it feels right.

Admitting my feelings isn't easy, but Tilly deserves truthfulness.

Tilly: Are the kids okay?

Me: Better than okay. Tate asked when you're coming for breakfast again.

I had a long talk with Tate when I put her to bed. She had a million questions about Tilly. The little thing is enamored of the cupcake-slinging Southern belle. I tried to be open and honest, but I didn't want to get her hopes up. I explained that Tilly and I are just friends, but I could tell by the way Tate was looking at me, she didn't believe a word of it.

Tilly: I hope we didn't confuse them.

Me: They're bored with me. They miss having a woman in the house.

I do everything I can and am both the mother and father, but there are some things I fail at no matter how hard I try.

Tilly: They just like my cupcakes.

Me: I like your cupcakes too.

I add a winky face to the message before I hit send.

Me: I have the day off tomorrow. Want to grab dinner?

Tilly: I'm running behind on the shop. Can I let you know later in the day?

There's a twinge in my chest, and for a second, I regret being so forward. But I know anything worth having is worth fighting for. Marissa was never one to let life pass by without seizing every moment. I need to at least try to carry out the wishes of my dying wife. I need to move forward instead of waiting for the few moments she comes to me in my dreams.

Me: What time are you going to be there?

Tilly: Probably nine. Why?

Me: I'll come help. That way you can't say no.

Tilly: I won't turn down your muscle.

Tilly: That sounded way dirtier than I intended.

I laugh so loud, I cover my mouth because if the kids wake up, I'll want to shoot myself.

Me: I am totally not offended.

Tilly: Phew. I was going to claim to be sleep-texting tomorrow if you were.

Me: I better let you get back to sleep.

Tilly: Get some rest too. You'll be no good to anyone if you're exhausted tomorrow.

Me: I'll see you at nine.

Tilly: Goodnight, Angelo.

Me: Night, Tilly.

I turn off the screen to my phone and sip the whiskey until sleep finally takes me again.

TILLY HANDS me a cup of badly needed coffee. "Did you get any sleep last night?" she asks as she sits down across from me.

"A little," I tell her, completely honest about my usual sleeping pattern.

"Dreams?" she asks.

"You have them?"

"About Mitchell?"

"Yeah," I say, surprised she knows exactly what I'm talking about.

She nods and wraps her hands around the warm mug. "I used to have them often, but lately, they're few and far between."

"I had one of Marissa last night."

"Ah," she murmurs. "That's why you couldn't sleep."

"I never really do. Well, not for long at least, but last night, she came to me."

"What did she say?" Tilly gazes at me from across the table. "If you don't mind my asking."

I shake my head. "Usually, we talk about the kids or it's a memory from our past, but last night was different."

"Different how?"

"It was as if she was saying goodbye." I glance down, staring at the wedding ring I haven't been able to take off my finger. "I can't shake the feeling that I'll never see her again. I always had my dreams."

Tilly reaches across the table and touches my arm. "I

138

dreamed of Mitchell last night too. It's been months since I've spoken to him."

"Are we normal?"

She nods. "Completely."

"Why did we both dream about them last night?"

Tilly shrugs with a pained smile. "Maybe because we both felt guilty about what happened."

"I didn't feel guilty kissing you, Tilly. Nothing has felt that right in so long."

"We feel guilty in our joy, Angelo."

I turn my hand over, capturing her fingers in mine. "You did make me happy," I admit, caressing her skin with my thumb. "Happier than I've been in a long time."

"Me too." She glances down to our interlocked hands. "It's easy to be with you. You don't judge me when I talk about Mitchell, and that's refreshing."

"I've experienced what you did, Tilly. I've lived through the sadness no one else can understand."

"I never dated because I didn't want someone to feel they were competing with Mitchell," she tells me, finally bringing her eyes back to mine.

"Many would find the memory too hard to compete with, but it's not a competition. If it were, it would be unwinnable."

Tilly reaches into her pocket and places an envelope on the table. "Roger gave this to me yesterday," she says, pushing it next to our hands.

I stare down at the ivory paper, noticing the ink smeared from tears. "Do you want me to read it?"

"I want to share it with you. Although the words are meant for me, I think they'll do you just as much good as they do me."

I touch the paper, running my fingers over her name. "Are you sure?"

She nods. "I'm going to prep a few things before we get started. Finish your coffee and read it."

"You don't want to stay with me?"

She shakes her head. "I can't. You'll understand why when you read it."

I give her a small smile before releasing her hand as she stands. "I won't be long."

She glances at me over her shoulder before disappearing into the kitchen, leaving me alone. I stare at the envelope as I drink my coffee, wondering if his words were meant to be shared. It feels almost sacrilegious for me to read his private thoughts and last words meant only for his wife.

I slowly unfold the letter and start to read.

My dearest Tilly,

There's not a moment in the eternal blackness that I'm not thinking of you. I never meant to leave you so soon, I planned to spend my life loving you and sheltering you from pain.

Roger was instructed to give this letter to you after you finally took a step forward, going on your first date.

While a part of me hopes you waited at least a few years, I pray you didn't wait too long.

There's nothing more important to me than your happiness. You are a creature that was never meant to be alone. You're strong, Tilly. A constant source of strength for me since the day I laid eyes on you. I need you to find that strength to move on, to go forward, and find your piece of happiness again.

I can never be fully at rest knowing you're alone. I've never loved someone as much as I loved you and never will again. But you're alive, Til. Don't forget that. Don't let your soul die along with my body. Let your heart experience joy and love again. Let yourself be free.

Move on knowing I'm with you, watching over you, and doing everything in my power for you to find that happiness. Don't think of a new relationship as throwing away a piece of us or cheating on the memory of our love.

I hope the man who has the good fortune to make you feel again is worthy and kind. Move forward without guilt or remorse. Live and love for me...for us.

There's no greater joy than love. Follow your dreams and your heart. Love fiercely. Don't be afraid when faced with the prospect of happiness again.

To honor my memory, to honor our vows, love again and live for me. Live for what we could've had and carry a piece of me with you, but don't let it take away the lifetime of happiness you deserve.

Find someone who will treat you as I did. Who will love you harder and deeper than me. Go forward without guilt, knowing I'm smiling down on you, finally able to have peace wherever I am.

I will always be yours, but you are no longer just mine to have. I love you more than you'll ever understand.

Move forward, baby.

Love again and never look back.

Eternally Yours,

Mitchell

CHAPTER FIFTEEN

TILLY

Strong arms wrap around me from behind as I stand at the prep table in the kitchen. He doesn't speak as he holds me and burrows his face in my neck. I close my eyes, missing the comfort of being in someone's arms without having to say a word.

He links his fingers near my stomach as his warm breath skids across my neck. "I'm sorry, Tilly," he whispers as he tightens his hold, pressing his front flush against my back. "I can't take your hurt away. I can't bring him back. The only thing I can do is be here for you, knowing everything you're feeling."

Emotion bubbles up inside me as tears start to form

in my eyes. "Do you feel lucky to have been able to say goodbye?"

He inhales and presses his face harder against my skin. "Sometimes," he admits. "Sometimes, I'm haunted by the memories of her trying to cling to life."

"I never got to say goodbye." I exhale as the tears fall down my face, wishing I could've touched Mitchell's warm skin one more time before he took his final breath. I cover Angelo's hands with mine and rest my head back against his chest. "The day he left, our goodbye was short and quick. I never thought he wouldn't come back."

"The letter was his goodbye, Tilly. He knows how much you love him. A man knows these things deep in his bones. We don't need to hear them in our final moments to know what we're leaving behind."

I close my eyes, sliding my hands up his arms to grip his biceps as I turn around. "There's so much left unsaid, Angelo. I never got to say them to his face. I lay across his flag-covered coffin, telling him everything I wanted him to know before they laid him to rest."

Angelo rocks gently, trying to calm me as I start to hyperventilate. "He heard you. There's no doubt in my mind he heard every word you spoke to him that day. He just couldn't talk back. He left you a letter as his final words, trying to tell you that he knew what you had was special."

"It was the greatest love," I whisper. "He was my

everything. My protector, my best friend, my love, my world."

"I know, baby. I know." There's nothing sexual in his tone. He's comforting me in a moment and a way no one else has been able to since Mitchell was alive. "Marissa was like the brightest star in the night's sky. She was everything I ever wanted. Even though I loved her and did everything in my power to protect her, I failed."

I turn in his arms, peering up at his tear-filled eyes, and hold his cheeks in my hands. "You loved her fiercely, Angelo. You did everything you could to protect and save her. This I know. But sometimes, the world has other plans, and no matter how hard we try to change things, there's no changing what's meant to be."

He rests his forehead against mine, hiding his eyes and his tears. "Marissa begged me to move on after she died. She couldn't leave until she made me promise not to be alone for the rest of my life. In her final moments, she thought of me and the kids more than herself."

"How were we so lucky to have them in our lives?"

He flattens his palms against the small of my back, and I crave his warmth. "I don't know, Tilly. I ask myself that question every day."

"You know why I haven't dated?"

Angelo tilts his head up just enough to see my eyes. "Why?"

"Because I didn't want to have to stop talking about

Mitchell. He's not an ex-anything, you know? I don't want another man to feel he's competing with him."

"I understand completely."

"But with you—" I wrap my arms around his waist, holding him tight "—I feel like I can say anything about Mitchell, and you won't judge or feel jealous."

"We were blessed with great love and cursed with even greater loss. If we can't share those feelings with someone, it'll never work. We'll never be able to move forward and continue living."

"Mitchell would've liked you, Angelo." I stare up into his crystal-blue eyes. "He'd like your quiet strength, your kind heart, and your ability to love completely."

"Marissa would've adored you too, Tilly. Your spirit is infectious, and you're sweeter than any cupcake you could ever bake."

I laugh softly, loving how he found a way to throw my cupcakes into the conversation. "Do you believe in fate?"

"I never did. I couldn't believe fate gave me Marissa and then snatched her away."

"It's hard to believe in anything when you lose someone so important."

"But if there's such a thing, I feel like you and I were destined to meet. We were meant to be here, in this time, helping each other heal."

I could easily fall for this man. His heart has an infinite capacity for love.

"Are we too broken to be together?" I whisper with my eyes locked with his.

He shakes his head and brushes his lips against my forehead. "I think we're too broken for other people, but together, we're whole."

I close my eyes and tighten my arms around his waist. "I haven't felt a moment's peace before being with you."

"I feel the same, Tilly."

We stand like that, embracing and just being for so long, I lose track of time. I'm lulled into a sense of peacefulness listening to the steady beat of his heart thumping in his chest underneath my ear.

"Do you still want to go out tonight?" he asks when the tears have finally stopped falling.

"I do," I say without opening my eyes or looking up. I'm so comfortable, I don't want to leave the serenity of his arms.

"Hello!" Betty calls from the front of the shop. "Anyone here?"

"Christ," Angelo mutters against my hair.

I laugh, loving the way his family is all up in each other's shit. It's something I never had but always wished I did.

"Back here." I release my hold on him and put some distance between us.

Betty comes stalking through the swinging door, dressed to the nines like she's about to head out for a swanky lunch date. "There you two are." She eyes us both like she knows something's going on.

She looks luminous in her bright green sweater and skinny jeans. For an older woman, she has a smoking hot body, looking at least ten years younger than her actual age.

"Hey, Ma." Angelo rubs the back of his neck.

"Hi, Betty."

"Hey, doll." She grabs my arms and pulls me toward her to kiss my cheek. "I know you two are busy, but I wanted to let you know we're having a family dinner tonight."

"But it's not Sunday, Ma."

Her red-painted lips flatten. "I know, but Vinnie's home for another day, and I want to do something special for him before he leaves."

"We have plans," he tells her.

She smiles. "You do. Dinner at my place at seven."

"But what about the bar?"

"I got it covered. That includes you, Tilly. I'm sure you could use a good home-cooked meal."

Angelo leans over, placing his mouth next to my ear. "Don't let her fool you. Her cooking is horrible," he whispers.

I stare at Betty with wide eyes as she glares at him. "I heard that, smartass. Daphne and Delilah are cooking."

"It'll be halfway edible, then." He laughs.

"It doesn't matter how good the food is. The most

important thing is that we're together as a family," his mother tells us.

"I know, Ma."

"Maybe we should just reschedule," I say.

Betty shakes her head. "No, dear. You're a part of us now."

"I am?" My mouth hangs open.

Betty grabs my shoulders. "You are, and Tate insisted I come over here and invite you."

"Oh," I whisper, caught off guard. "Can I bring anything?"

"Just yourself."

Angelo's behind me and silent.

"Seven o'clock. Got it?" she reminds us like we'd actually forget.

"We'll be there, Ma," he tells her.

She stares at us for a moment. "You two would make beautiful children," she says out of left field.

I practically choke on my own spit and start to cough uncontrollably.

Angelo places his hand on my shoulder and squeezes. "Ma, bring it down a notch."

"I'm just stating the obvious." She shrugs. "Do with it as you will. Now, I'm off. I'm meeting Mrs. Onorato for lunch at Piatto."

"'Dish'?" I ask, wondering who the hell would name their restaurant "Dish."

"Yes, dear. You know Italian?"

"I spent a year in Italy with Mitchell. He was stationed there. I picked up a thing or two."

"Oh. I like her." His mother winks.

"Aren't you late?"

"Seven," she says again as she pushes the swinging door and disappears into the front of the shop. Neither of us speaks until the sound of her high heels fades.

"She's intense." I can't stop myself from laughing as I turn around to face him.

"The entire family is crazy as fuck."

"I've met them."

"You haven't seen them all in action." He pulls me back into an embrace.

"I always wanted a big family. I'm excited to have dinner with them."

"You sure? I can cancel, and we can go out alone."

I shake my head, wanting nothing more than to spend a quiet evening with his family. "I'm sure, Angelo. They're a part of you."

"The crazy part." He pulls me closer, holding me so tightly, I never want him to let me go.

"Being normal is never fun."

"Be careful what you ask for. I worry they may be a little too much to handle all at once. At least so soon."

"It's always better to rip the Band-Aid off quickly."

At least, that's what I tell myself. I'd be lying if I didn't say I was a little nervous about tonight. I've met them all, and from what I can tell, they're everything a family should be.

CHAPTER SIXTEEN

ANGELO

I SLIDE my hands up and down Tilly's arms as we stand outside the bar. "This is your last chance to escape."

Tilly turns and stares through the windows. "I think it'll be okay."

She has no idea what she's walking into. My family as individuals are good. At least, for the most part. Put them all together in one room, especially with a newcomer, and shit can tend to get a little crazy.

"Just remember. If it becomes too much or you feel overwhelmed, let me know, and we'll leave."

"Too much for you or for me?" She laughs.

I lean forward and grab her chin with my fingertips. "I like your sass."

She bites her bottom lip and smirks. "I like your ass," she replies, and I can only shake my head.

"You'll fit right in with this bunch."

"Thank you," she says, staring at me with those green eyes that render me speechless.

I search her gaze. "For what?"

I should be the one thanking her for being here with me tonight even though she doesn't have to be.

"For making me feel wanted."

"Tilly." I bring my lips closer to hers. "I can't explain all the things you make me feel."

There's nothing more to say. This woman has made me feel more alive than I have in the last three years. I want to lose myself in her.

I bend forward, placing my lips on hers ever so lightly. The kiss is sweet, pure, and everything I'm feeling. She kisses me back, gripping my arms tightly. Our hot breath mingles with the cold night air as I back away and try to catch my breath.

"Don't do that."

I raise an eyebrow. "Don't kiss you?"

"Not like that. Not when we have to spend the evening with your family."

I laugh and kiss her forehead. "I promise I won't kiss you again until we're alone."

She snuggles into me, wrapping her fingers around my collar. "I could stay like this all night."

I'm just about to ditch my family when there's a knock at the window. My ma's face is pressed against the glass, and she's gawking at us. "Get in here," she says, but her voice is muffled by the street noise and the music from inside the bar.

Tilly snorts. "Guess we're taking too long."

"My ma is so nosy."

"It's nice." She looks up at me with a sweet, innocent smile.

"I'll remind you of that in a few hours." I open the front door to a very impatient Betty.

"Everyone's waiting for you two, while you play kissy-face on the street." Ma's tapping her foot with her arms crossed.

"Kissy-face?" I repeat, unable to stop laughing as we follow her through the busy bar.

"Come on. The food's almost ready." She motions for us to follow her up the stairs as she moves faster than she usually does. "You know your brother. He's always starving."

"They're all overdramatic," I tell Tilly as I have her walk in front of me and behind my mother.

"They're here," Ma announces as we step foot on the landing to her apartment. "I found them making out on the street."

"Way to go, bro." Vinnie winks.

Tilly blushes at my brother's dumbass comment and my mother's overstatement of what she saw downstairs. Maybe in my mother's time, making out meant a brief kiss on the lips, but not in this century.

Ma grabs Tilly by the arm, pulling her toward the

living room and away from me. "Come, let me introduce you."

She's getting the Gallo baptism by fire without any
tiptoeing into the horde.

I collapse into the kitchen chair next to Vinnie and
shrug off my jacket, but I keep my eyes trained on Tilly.

He leans into my personal space. "You're a goner."

"Maybe." I don't even look at him and I don't pause,
but I'm only being partially truthful.

"There's no maybe about that shit. You can't take
your eyes off her."

I grunt.

"You going to make her yours or pussy out?"

I give him a side-eye. "You still bed-hoppin'?"

"Well, duh. I'm a senior. I'm all about the pussy."

I shake my head. "You got to grow up sometime."

"Next year when I'm playing pro ball," he says like,
somehow, that makes any sense. "But again, are you
going to date that chick or what? She's a primo piece
of ass."

I give him an icy stare. "Do not ever, under any
circumstances, refer to her as a primo piece of ass."

He jerks his head back before he gives me a shitty
smirk. "Yep. I knew it."

"What are you two arguing about?" Lucio sits down
across from us, almost blocking my view of Tilly.

"Her." Vinnie ticks his chin toward the living room.

Lucio rubs his chin as he stares at me. "Did you
make her yours yet?"

"No."

"Why not?" Lucio shrugs.

"It's complicated."

"Brother—" Lucio starts to say, but I cut him off.

"I know. I know. But there's more than just my past we're working through. We're taking things slow."

"You can take it as slow as you want, but you better lock that shit down."

He's repeating the words I said to him about Delilah. I knew that crap would come back to haunt me someday.

"I will," I grumble.

"I mean it, Angelo. Lock it down before you lose it," he tells me again, pointing at me like I'm not hearing his words.

"I said we're going slow."

"I'm not saying you need to sleep with her, but you need to make sure she isn't sleeping with anyone else."

I level him with my gaze. "She's not like that."

Lucio lifts his hands in the air. "I wasn't saying she was, but you both need the security and certainty."

What he's saying isn't wrong. With our pasts, we needed everything clear-cut so there's no chance either of us would feel a sense of insecurity or worry. The last thing I want is for Tilly to even think another woman had a shot at me.

Every night at work, I get at least a half-dozen phone numbers. Each and every one of them ends up in the trash because there's no way I'm dating a customer.

While I'm a man with needs, I'm also a father and have to think of my children before my dick.

Tilly's chatting with Delilah and Daphne on the couch and paying no attention to me. I'm fine with it. I want her to feel comfortable around my family. If she doesn't, there wouldn't be a future for us.

"You better take her on a date," Ma says as she walks back into the kitchen.

"I was taking her on one tonight before you invited us here."

"Well." Ma shakes her head. "Tomorrow, then."

"Sure, because I have nothing else to do. Who needs to spend time with the kids?"

She puts her hands on her hips and narrows her eyes. "Don't sass me, mister."

Fuck. It doesn't matter how old I am, Ma still treats me like a little kid. She'll turn on a dime, reminding me that she's the boss of all of us…forever.

"Tilly's trying to open a business, and I have two little ones. It's not easy to find free nights to go on dates. That's all I'm saying."

She grabs the oven mitts, turning her back to us. "Why don't you invite her over for dinner?"

"I don't want to confuse the kids."

"Sweetheart," she says in a sugary voice like she always does when she doesn't agree. "Tate already found her sleeping on your couch, and she was fine. It's just a meal. People have to eat."

"Delilah and I can watch the kids," Lucio offers,

finally understanding the joys of fatherhood when trying to get laid or you know…do anything. "They can even spend the night."

"Can you handle that?" I ask, knowing that's a mighty big ask.

"What's two more? It's already mass chaos at our place. The only thing I can promise is that they'll come back alive, but everything else is a crapshoot."

Ma touches my shoulder. "Do it, baby. You deserve some happiness and a night off."

Lucio watches me, waiting. I can never thank my brother enough for what he did for me after Marissa died. He took the kids off my hands more times than I can count, sheltering them from the spiral I couldn't escape and the depths of my depression.

"I'll take you up on the offer, brother, but only if I can return the favor."

"Fuck yeah." He groans. "I'm so exhausted, I just want to sleep an entire night through."

"This is why I don't settle down with just one honey." Vinnie picks at the label on his beer bottle. "You two make adulthood seem like the shittiest thing ever."

"You keep sticking that thing into whatever has tits, and you're going to end up with a kid of your own real quick."

He downs his beer and wipes his mouth with the back of his hand. "Please. I always wear a rubber."

"Well, at least you're smart enough for that," Lucio mumbles under his breath.

"Angelo." Daphne clears her throat as she walks into the kitchen with her arm linked with Tilly's. "This one's a keeper."

Tilly snorts. "You're too nice, Daphne."

I laugh. "Most people wouldn't use that word to describe her."

"Well, you're an asshole too," Daphne says and sticks out her tongue like we're twelve.

"I'm passionate." I wink at Tilly.

Tilly sucks her lips into her mouth, biting back the laughter.

"Anyway." Daphne ignores my comment like she usually does. "We girls are going shopping this weekend. Ma, you too."

Ma perks up, turning around with the roaster in her hands. "I'm invited?" She seems shocked, but she's always included in everything "the girls" do.

"For sure." Tilly nods. "I've never had a girls' day."

"Oh lord," I mutter and glance toward the ceiling.

"It'll be fabulous. I'm so excited." Delilah claps her hands, always down for whatever shenanigans Daphne can cook up.

Leo comes up behind Daphne and wraps his arms around her waist. "The entire day is my treat," he announces. "No expense is too great for my *bella*."

"Well, I don't know what to say." Ma's at a loss for words, which never happens. The woman has shit to say about anything and everything, but Leo's all-expenses-paid shopping spree has her lips locked. She just stands there, holding the pot roast, and gawks at Leo.

Tilly's beaming. Absolutely radiant as she stands next to my sister, staring at the girls.

"Why don't we go Sunday since we're having dinner tonight?" Daphne asks Ma.

"Sunday, it is." Ma nods, finally setting the roaster on top of the stove. "This worked out perfectly."

"Are you sure you're okay with this, Tilly?" Daphne asks.

Tilly nods and looks to me. "Is your brother?"

I lift my hands, happy to see her happy. "Whatever makes you happy. Go enjoy yourself for the day. You deserve it."

I can already tell my family's taken a liking to Tilly, just as much as I have. It's time I take my own advice and lock that shit down, making her mine and putting all doubt to rest.

CHAPTER SEVENTEEN

TILLY

THE SUN'S SHINING, and the sky is a brilliant blue for the first time in what seems like months. Birds are chirping above me, sounding just as happy as I feel to know spring's right around the corner.

I spread one blanket on the grass and wrap another around me before sitting. "I needed to talk to you."

I grab the broken twigs, gathering them into a neat pile to keep myself from falling apart. I can't bring myself to look up, keeping my eyes focused on the wilted grass near the edge of the blanket instead.

"I met someone." I pull the blanket tighter around me as the wind kicks up. "You'd like him."

I hang my head, letting my eyes fill with tears. I've

never been able to talk to him without crying, and today's no different. I thought today would be easier. Moving on is supposed to be. Or at least, that's what I've been told.

"He's honorable and kind, just like you, Mitchell." I take a deep breath, finally letting myself look at his headstone.

"Roger gave me your letter the other day." I pause, wishing he could talk back or I could get some sign that he's at least listening.

I never thought much about life after death until Mitchell died, but since that moment, I'm always searching for him in the faint sounds in the stillness of the night.

"I haven't been able to move on. In my heart, I'll always be your wife even if you're not here to be by my side."

I pull his letter from my pocket and unfold the paper.

"Some days I can't breathe when I realize this isn't all some cruel joke and that you're really gone."

My eyes scan the paper as my fingers trace his handwriting. "I've waited five years to wake up from the nightmare, Mitchell. I know you're never coming back."

I don't think I've ever said those words out loud before now. They were too painful. They still are, but somehow, I know they must be said.

"Angelo makes me feel alive again," I tell Mitchell,

but a part of me feels guilty for even the smallest amount of joy.

"This isn't a goodbye, love. I could never say goodbye to you no matter how many years or how infinite the distance that separates us."

I touch the headstone, flattening my palm next to his name. "I'm following the wishes of the letters you've left behind. I'm moving forward with my life. You should see the cupcake shop. You would've gotten a kick out of it, but I'm following my dreams."

Jesus. I'm blabbering. I'm jumping around from topic to topic because focusing too much on Angelo doesn't seem right, even if Mitchell says it's okay.

"I'll make you proud," I promise him.

I sit there for an hour, cleaning away the winter debris from his gravesite and polishing his headstone. I used to come here weekly, but with planning the shop and the extremely cold winter, I haven't been here in a month.

"I love you." I climb to my feet. I back away, staring at his gravesite as a reminder of what I lost and my past. I know I need to move on, following the wishes Mitchell left behind for me.

"I will love you until my dying breath."

"WHEN ARE YOU SEEING HIM AGAIN?" Roger never beats around the bush. He picks at a cupcake, eating the bottom before the top because he likes to save the best part until the end.

"Tomorrow. We're having dinner." I take the wrapper from his hand, trying to stay busy instead of focusing on our first real date.

We told each other pizza the other night counted, but we both knew it was a lie. I wasn't nervous, knowing we were only friends, even if the chemistry was off the charts and the attraction undeniable.

"Where's he taking you?"

"He's cooking."

Roger's eyes widen. "The man knows you're a baker, right?"

I motion toward the kitchen, a place Angelo's been in at least a half a dozen times. "Uh, yeah. I think he got the message."

"I don't cook for you."

I snort. "You're kind of a shit cook. You're really great at picking the right restaurant, though."

Roger hops up on the table, making himself comfortable. "What's he making?"

I shrug and go on mixing the latest batch of blueberry frosting. "He said it's a surprise."

"Are you going to shave everything?"

I gawk at Roger. "Are we really having this conversation?"

He nods. "You need to be prepared for all possibilities. Hell, get a Brazilian."

I point the spatula at him. The man falls to his knees

if he gets a paper cut. "Why don't you get the hair ripped off your asshole and then we'll talk, 'kay?"

Roger shivers. "Men aren't meant to be hairless."

"Neither is my pussy, buddy. I'll trim."

"It's not the seventies, babe. Bush is not in, and no man wants a mouth full of fur."

I shoot him a look over my mixing bowl. "How would you know?"

He gags. "I know when I get a hair stuck in my throat, it takes everything in me not to hurl right on the man."

"Wait." I stop what I'm doing and give him my full attention. "Do guys have hairy dicks?"

He laughs. "I've seen a few, but when their shit isn't manscaped and it's a mess down there, it's an immediate no for me."

"So, you just walk away? Just like that?"

He licks the top layer of frosting from his cupcake and closes his eyes. "This shit is bananas."

"It's blueberry," I correct him. "Answer my question."

"I meant it's amazing."

"Roger."

"Fine. I don't walk away when they have hair thicker than the densest forest. They can happily suck my dick, but I'm not returning the favor."

"You're a pig." I fling a glob of frosting in his direction.

"Babe." He laughs. "A pig wouldn't care what a

man has going on down there. They'd suck him off like he contains the last drop of water on earth. But me." He touches his chest. "I'm a cock connoisseur, and I'll only put the best in my mouth."

"Fuck. You're sick."

"What was the last cock you saw besides my brother's?"

I busy myself, avoiding answering that one because Roger would flip his lid if I told him the truth. There's no way I'm divulging my sex life before Mitchell. No way in hell.

"Tilly," he says. "The last cock."

God, it's so embarrassing. I can barely bring myself to even think about the answer, let alone voice it.

"Wait." He hops off the table and stalks toward me, stopping just a few feet away. "Don't say it."

"I'm not." I stare down at the blue frosting turning in the bowl.

"Did you see another cock besides Mitchell's?"

"I've seen plenty."

He puts his hands down on the steel island, and I can feel the weight of his stare without even looking up. "How many cocks have you seen?"

"Tons," I say, way overstating the true reality.

"In person?"

"Well, yeah." I mean, I saw them with my own eyes, but they may have been on the computer or television. Mitchell's is the only dick I've actually seen live and in living color.

"Oh fuck. You were a virgin before Mitchell, weren't you?"

I glance up, narrowing my gaze. "What's so wrong with that?"

"Nothing. Nothing at all. Not even a handy or two to some poor schmuck in high school?"

I shake my head.

"Thirty years old and only one cock." He says it like it's the most unbelievable thing he's ever heard.

"Yep."

"Do you remember what to do?"

I drop the spatula in the mixing bowl and hang my head, trying not to laugh or cry. I'm on the verge of both, but I can't seem to figure out which one best suits how I feel.

"I think I remember my way around a dick, Roger. They're not that complicated."

"True."

"Plus, your brother never seemed to complain."

"Eh," Roger mutters. "When you love someone, nothing else matters."

"Are you saying I was a bad lay?"

"I'm saying you can do no wrong. Calm your shit, woman. Just promise me you'll be prepared for your date."

I rub my forehead with the back of my hand and sigh. "What if I can't do it?"

"It's like riding a bike. If you have trouble, just let him take the lead."

"No, Roger. I'm talking about what if I freeze up and can't. Mitchell's the only man I've ever been with, and what if my mind isn't ready to take the next step?"

"Tilly." He touches my arms, always comforting me. "If Angelo's any kind of man, he'll wait as long as you need. If he doesn't, I'll kick his ass so that he'll never look at you again."

"Don't be an asshole." I smack his chest. "I really like this guy."

"Don't worry about anything, babe. When the time's right, it'll happen. Just follow your heart, and you can never go wrong."

CHAPTER EIGHTEEN

ANGELO

TATE'S BEEN PUTTING on a ballerina performance for the last thirty minutes, giving absolutely zero shits that I'm trying to get ready for my date. She's spinning around the living room, wearing the purple tutu my mother bought her for Christmas, pulling out all the stops to get me to change my mind.

"Why can't I stay, Daddy?"

The minute she heard Tilly was coming over, she started to whine. She loves Uncle Lucio and Aunt Delilah and is usually thrilled to be going to their house, but not tonight. Not when Cupcake Tilly's going to be in the house.

"It's an adult night, baby."

"I'll stay in my room." She does this thing with her lip like it's going to make me change my mind.

"We both know that's not true."

"I promise."

"You'll have fun with Uncle Lucio. Let Daddy have a little time with Tilly."

"Are you two going to fall asleep on the couch again?"

I shake my head. "No, sweetheart."

I wouldn't mind another night of Tilly in my arms. I forgot how peaceful it was to sleep with someone. The kids are hell at night when they crawl in my bed, kicking me like I'm in their way and not the other way around.

Lucio walks through the door and catches sight of Tate. "I see we're still on the ballet kick."

Tate screams and runs toward Lucio, jumping into his arms. "Uncle." She giggles as he tickles her ribs. "Stop."

He holds her tightly, giving her a moment to catch her breath. "Are you ready for some fun, squirt?"

"Can we have cookies?"

"Sure."

"Can we have cake?"

"I don't know."

"What do you mean, you don't know?"

Lucio looks at me, clearly seeking help, but I only shrug and continue to clear the dinner table of their coloring books and crayons.

"Dude." He points to Tate as she pouts in his arms. "Where does she put it?"

"No idea, man, but the kid will eat you out of house and home."

"Uncle Lucio." She grabs his face, and I know what's coming. She's going to turn on the cute little girl charm, wrapping him further around her finger.

"What, doll?" He pushes her brown hair over her shoulder.

She leans closer, and their noses almost touch. "If you get me cake, I promise to be a good girl." She mushes his cheeks together. "Please."

Man, this kid makes it damn near impossible to say no to her. I struggle with it at times, but her uncles… They have zero ability to deny her anything when she pulls out all the stops.

"Gimme a kiss," Lucio tells her with his fish lips. "And we'll stop and get cake for dessert."

Tate's eyes widen like she's shocked. She's not. She knew exactly what she was doing with my brother. She keeps her hold on his face as she gives him a sloppy kiss on the lips, but it's only for a second. She wiggles, trying to break free of his arms. "I have to get my bag," she tells him as she pushes against his chest.

"And your brother," I tell her as her feet touch the floor, and she takes off down the hallway, skipping because she got exactly what she wanted.

Lucio's a sucker. We all are. Tate knows it. I know it. But somehow, my family keeps falling for her tricks.

Lucio rubs the back of his neck, laughing. "She just played me, didn't she?"

"Like a pro."

"When she hits puberty, you better lock her in her room."

I laugh, but the thought's crossed my mind more than once. I'm already pissed at the first fucker who's going to lay his hands on my kid, professing to love her forever, when he's really just a dick with legs.

Lucio leans against the counter, watching me as I enter panic mode, shoving shit wherever I can find room.

"Everything ready for Tilly?"

"Food's in the oven, and I cleaned, so…yeah." I glance around the bottom level, amazed at how clean my place looks. With two kids, having a surface free of toys is completely unheard of. But Tilly saw it in all its glory the other night and didn't seem to flinch.

"We'll keep the kids as long as you want. Don't rush on our account. Delilah already has plans for them tomorrow afternoon."

"You don't have to do that. I can pick them up early."

Lucio flattens his lips. "Slow your roll, Jimmy Dean."

"What the fuck are you talking about?"

"You know. The sausage?" he asks like I'm a complete idiot for not understanding. "Never mind. Just enjoy some you time."

I nod. "That's the plan."

"And don't forget to…"

"Yeah. Yeah. Yeah." I wave him off.

"Lock it up tight, brother."

Tate comes barreling into the living room with two backpacks, one on her back and the other in her hand, and she's pulling Brax by the collar with her free hand. "We're ready," she says like she can't get away from me fast enough.

Lucio grabs the backpack from her hand and stares at her other hand until she gets the message to let go of her brother. "How does DeLuca's sound?"

Tate squeals. "Perfect. Can we get Cassata cake?"

"I'm sure they sell it by the slice."

I laugh because I know a slice is never enough for my little monster.

She puts her hands on her hips and furrows her brows. "I mean, the whole cake."

He jerks his head back, and again, he looks at me for help. "Really?"

"She will stab you with her fork if you try to take a bite of her cake. You're safer if you buy the whole damn thing," I tell him, giving him a warning because my girl is off the charts crazy about her sweets.

He gawks at her. "We gotta talk about your eating habits, kid."

She pulls at his hand and moves toward the doorway, barely looking at me. "Bye, Daddy."

I grab Brax, giving him a giant hug before he latches on to Lucio's other hand. "Be a good little man."

"I got this," Lucio tells me, but he looks more like they've got him than the other way around.

I watch through the window as Lucio piles the kids into his new extended cab pickup. That was the closest thing he'd get to a family car, but it's an improvement over his old motorcycle.

I have exactly one hour until Tilly arrives. That's just enough time to finish tidying up, shower, and get my shit under control before she walks through the door.

I feel like we had a breakthrough the other day after our talk in her kitchen and dinner at my parents'. She fit right in, and in true Gallo fashion, they welcomed her into the fold.

Now it's my turn to make sure she knows for sure that I want more than friendship. There's more between us than attraction. We're separate halves of the same broken heart, searching for peace in a world that no longer seems to make sense.

TILLY KICKS OFF HER SHOES, making herself more comfortable on the couch next to me. She turns, one arm propped up on the cushion and the other hand holding a glass of white wine. "I needed an evening like this."

I face her, letting my knee touch hers. It's so high

school, but I'm trying to find my single guy groove again. I knew dating would be hard. Marissa and I had been together for so long, I was really clueless when it came to anything besides what she liked. Even then, my moves weren't entirely smooth, but none of that mattered.

I rub my hand down my leg, trying to remain calm for the big talk I know needs to happen. "You're going to be so busy once the shop opens."

I sound like an idiot. Like an insecure moron, already justifying why she may not call again after tonight. All the vibes are there. We click. There's chemistry. We share a disconnected yet similar past. But what if… What if I ask her to be mine, and she runs the other way, scared as fuck to move on and unable to let go of her husband?

She touches my knee. "It'll be crazy, but I won't let it rule my life. There are other things that are much more important." She's staring at me as she says those words. "I've learned that time is the most precious thing we have, and although the cupcake shop has been my dream for so long, I realize I want more out of life."

"Tilly." I move closer, placing my hand over hers. "I want to talk to you about something important."

She leans over and places her wine on the coffee table. "Of course. What's wrong?"

Reaching up, I tuck a lock of hair behind her ear and leave my hand on her cheek instead of pulling away. "We have a connection, yeah?"

She nods, tilting her head and moving into my touch.

"I truly feel like we were meant to be here, in this moment, at this time in our lives. You came into my world for a reason, and I'm undeniably and inextricably drawn to you. When you're near, I feel at peace for the first time in longer than I can remember."

"Me too," she whispers, gazing at me in the dim candlelight.

"I want no one else in this world as much as I want you. We can move slow, but I want there to be no doubt about my intentions. I want you as my own. Only mine and no one else's."

The corner of her mouth touches my thumb. "Are you mine, then?"

"No one else's."

She slides her leg away and moves her body within inches of mine. "I'm falling for you, Angelo. Falling hard and fast."

My heart sputters at her confession. "I know it's crazy, but I feel the same way. The moment I laid eyes on you and heard you tell off that mixer, I knew I wanted you."

She leans forward, taking me by surprise when she climbs into my lap. My hands are on her back in an instant, holding her tightly. "Say you're mine."

She presses her chest flush against me, bringing her lips close to mine. In the faint light, her eyes are dark, but the fire within burns brightly. "I want to be yours,

Angelo."

I lean forward, tightening my grip on her body, and press my mouth to hers. She tastes of the sweetest white wine as my tongue brushes against her bottom lip. She's intoxicating. Pure and simple.

She slides her hands up my arms, settling them around my neck as I deepen the kiss. The need to explore her body almost overwhelms my restraint for the slow, controlled pace I'd promised. The fact that she's moving around on top of my cock doesn't make anything easier.

She fists her fingers in the back of my hair and swipes her tongue in my mouth, tangling with mine. Sweet baby Jesus, I want this woman. I want her more than I've wanted anything or anyone in so long.

She's like coming home again.

CHAPTER NINETEEN

TILLY

His body is like liquid lava against mine. I've missed the warmth of a man and being wrapped in strong arms. He's stolen my breath almost completely with the way he kisses me, passionate and with purpose.

"Angelo," I whisper against his lips, hoping I don't scare him away with what I'm about to say.

He opens his ice-blue eyes and stares at me with pure and utter lust. "Is this too much?"

I shake my head and lean back so I can see his face and not just his eyes. "I need to tell you something and ask something too."

He flattens his palms against my back, keeping me close like I'm going to try to run. "Ask me anything."

"Well." I glance down at his chest, unable to look him in the eyes. "I have never been with anyone besides Mitchell."

The warmth of his hand is gone, and my stomach flutters for a moment because maybe that was too much information in the heat of the moment.

"Tilly." His fingers are on my chin, lifting my face to meet his gaze. "Don't worry. We can just kiss."

I almost burst into tears at the sweetness of this man, but I swallow them down, determined to get over my fear. "I don't want that."

His lips part as he sucks in a breath, maybe caught more off guard by my last words.

"I want you, Angelo. I want to be with you. I want to know what it feels like to have your skin pressed against mine."

He slides his hand against my cheek and curls his fingers around my neck. "Are you sure?" His beautiful blue eyes search my face.

I reach between my legs, cupping his stiff cock in my palm. "Completely."

He closes his eyes and takes a deep breath. "I haven't made love to a woman in three years, Tilly. I've got to take this slow." He gazes at me with a hunger I've never seen before.

For a moment, I'm shocked, but I shouldn't be. From everything I know about Angelo, he's thoughtful in everything he does. It shouldn't surprise me that his approach to sex isn't any different.

He moves his one hand to my hip and pulls me in for a kiss with the other. "If you want to stop, just say the word."

"I don't. I want you." The words are barely out of my mouth before his lips crash down on mine.

I slip my fingers under his shirt, running them along the dips and curves of his abs as they flex under my touch. The man is soft and hard in all the right places.

"I need you," he says against my lips before he stands, taking me with him.

I wrap my legs around his waist, clinging to him as he walks toward the hallway with me in his arms. The kiss isn't frantic, but it is passionate and intense. His tongue tangles with mine in a delicate dance of need and lust.

He covers me with his body as he lays me on the bed, careful not to crush me under the weight of his massive frame. I'm not sure I've ever felt so small compared to another human being as I do in this moment with him hovering above me.

His bicep ripples next to my head as he lifts himself up on one arm and uses the other to pull his shirt over his head. In the faint glow of the streetlights shining through the window, I can see every muscle on his chest and shoulders as if they were carved out of the hardest stone.

I widen my eyes. The man is literally built like a Roman god without an ounce of fat anywhere on his body. "Jesus," I mutter, not meaning to say that out loud but doing it anyway.

"This isn't right."

My stomach sinks.

Fuck. Why did I have to open my big mouth?

I lock my ankles behind his ass, not wanting him to stop. "No, I'm okay." I push myself up on my elbows, getting a better look at his killer body. "Keep going."

Angelo laughs. "No, I want to undress you slowly."

"Oh." The moment of panic passes, and I release my death grip on his ass.

"Stand," he tells me like I don't really have an option, which, somehow, is okay with me.

He climbs off the bed first, and I follow the motion of each and every muscle rippling on his torso with my eyes. I just lie there, half upright, gawking at him like I've never seen a naked chest before. I have, but not one quite like his.

I don't move until he finally motions for me to take his hand. I mean, who can move, let alone think, when there's all that muscle flexing in such beautiful harmony? Clearly not me.

"I'm sorry." My face heats as I come face-to-face with his pecs. I want to reach out and touch them, testing to see if they're as hard as they look. "I've just never seen so much muscle on one man."

He smiles but doesn't laugh. Jesus. I feel like a complete moron. I would give my dorky high school self a run for her money in the awkward sex retelling of my life.

"Just relax." His head dips forward, and his lips brush against my neck just below my jaw.

My skin breaks out in goose bumps, and my eyes roll back. The volume of pleasure this man can deliver with a simple kiss is mind-boggling. I'm putty in his hands at this point, and there's no turning back. My neck has always been my weakness.

When his fingers slide under the spaghetti straps of the black top I'm wearing, my breath hitches and butterflies fill my stomach. No man has seen me naked in five years. Parts of my body no longer lie where they used to, and gravity, along with age, has clearly taken its toll.

"You're beautiful," he whispers against my skin as if he senses my fear.

As the first strap slides down my arm, his lips disappear from my neck. Our eyes lock as the strap moves past my finger, exposing one breast. I expect him to look down, but he doesn't as his hand moves to the second strap and lingers.

"Breathe, Tilly."

I gasp, not realizing I'd actually stopped breathing. "I'm sorry." I swallow, focusing on his eyes and nothing else to help keep my fear at bay.

The cold air drifts across my breasts as the second strap falls off my shoulder, leaving me bare. His hand slides around my back, just above my ass, and he pulls me flush against him.

I melt into his warmth, reveling in the softness of his skin against mine. I've missed this. Missed the connection to another human being only nakedness can give.

His mouth crashes down against my lips as his fingers slowly inch down my back, finding the zipper to my skirt. I give him my mouth willingly, wanting nothing more than to taste his sweet lips.

For a moment, I think of Roger, thankful I followed his advice and shaved everything. I wasn't sure where the night would lead us, but in my heart, I was hoping to feel Angelo's body pressed against mine just like it is now.

My stomach flutters as the teeth of my zipper separate and my skirt falls to my feet. I'm completely naked, stepping outside my comfort zone and going without panties for the first time in years.

My heart's racing as he grips my ass, pulling my body closer to his and, by default, pressing his cock against me. I'm winded by the thickness and length, forgetting exactly how it feels to be filled, but excited to be reminded. I almost thought I'd never have sex again, destined to be celibate forever.

My fingers find his jeans in the darkness, working the zipper down in quick fashion and tugging at the sides of his waistband until his cock springs free.

His lips leave mine, and I open my eyes as he backs away. We're both naked with nothing separating us.

"God, Tilly." He finally lets his gaze wander over my naked flesh. "You're perfect."

I drink him in as a whole before my eyes take him in piece by piece. Wide shoulders. Insane amount of muscles. Thick thighs. Huge cock. The man's body was created to be worshiped. "You're a whole lotta man, Angelo."

His cock twitches, catching my eye again. Like I hadn't noticed the enormous size of the damn thing moments ago. To say it's impressive is an understatement.

"I'll be gentle," he promises.

I'm not entirely sure I want his gentleness after five years of absolute abstinence.

He steps forward and closes the space between us before grabbing my waist. "You're mine, Tilly. I'll always protect you and will never hurt you."

As soon as he says those words, a peace unlike anything I've ever felt before washes over me.

"Make love to me," I whisper into the still night air, gazing into the blue eyes of the man I'm quickly falling in love with.

He guides me toward the bed, covering my body with his again before sliding between my legs. "You're shaking." He runs his lips across my skin near my collarbone.

"Kiss me." I pull his face down to mine and take his mouth with such intensity, I leave no doubt in his mind or my own what I want.

He glides his hand across my skin, brushing near my nipple and sending shock waves throughout my entire body. I arch my back, craving his touch and wanting more of the delicious pleasure only his fingertips can deliver.

His lips slip from mine, following the same path his fingertips just took. I moan, unable to hold back when his warm, wet tongue touches the side of my nipple. I dig my fingernails into his shoulders, begging for more of his mouth and wanting all the pleasure he has to offer.

I press his cock against my aching pussy as I wrap my legs around his hips and lock our bodies together. "I want you," I whisper as my fingers find the hard planes of his back. "I can't wait any longer."

He lifts his head and stares up my body. "Don't rush this, baby. Don't rush me or your pleasure," he says before he lowers his head over my other breast.

CHAPTER TWENTY

ANGELO

My mouth covers her pussy as she shakes uncontrollably in the bed. I hum my approval, adding to the overwhelming sensation she's no doubt feeling.

"Oh God. Oh God," she calls out as I swipe my tongue across her clit, and her fingers wrap around the comforter at her side. "Yes!"

She's loud, and I love that about her. There's no timid Tilly, scared to ask for what she wants or too bashful to let me know when I've hit the right spots. There's never any guessing with her, even when it comes to sex.

I smile around her clit, sucking her sensitive skin harder than before. She starts chanting a language I've never heard before, rocking her hips and pushing her pussy against my face.

"I'm coming," she says, almost singing the words. "Oh fuck."

Her words spur me on, making me lick quicker and suck harder until her body's quaking against the sheets and she's gasping for air. I keep my eyes locked on her, looking at her naked body as her chest heaves.

She doesn't speak, trying to catch her breath as she melts into the mattress. I slide between her legs, lining up my cock with her inviting pussy. Her knees fall to the bed, opening to me. I slide one hand under her ass and guide my cock slowly inside her with the other.

She peers up with her green eyes, cheeks flushed. I'm moving slowly, easing myself inside her gradually because the last thing I want to do is have this be over before I have a chance to really get started.

I close my eyes, the sweet ecstasy her pussy delivers almost pushing me over the edge. Go slow, I tell myself. I need this. I want this. There's a time for fast, but now isn't it.

I pull my hips back before thrusting forward with a little more force. I practically lose it, but I rebound as my body stills. Leaning forward, I take her nipple in my mouth, loving the way her pussy clamps down around my shaft.

Twisting my hips, I grind into her, pressing against her clit. Slowly, and almost to the point of torture, I move again. I grip her ass with one hand as I hold myself up with the other, staring down at the woman I've quickly fallen in love with.

Our eyes are locked on each other's as I rock into her over and over again, keeping a slow, steady rhythm. Her legs wrap around my waist, and she locks her ankles against my ass. "Deeper," she whispers.

I rock upward, forcing my cock deeper inside her, knowing I can't last much longer. It's impossible with the way her body feels wrapped around my dick and the length of time it's been since I've felt anything this spectacular.

Tilly moves with me, shaking in my arms as her breathing grows more erratic with each thrust. My entire body's on fire as the orgasm begins to take hold, making it impossible for me to stop.

I tilt her ass upward, changing the angle and pushing my pelvis against her clit. Within seconds, she's crying out, digging her fingernails into my biceps as the orgasm builds inside each of us.

I thrust harder, moving faster than before, and chase the orgasm for us both. I squeeze my eyes shut, and colors explode behind my lids like a grand finale on the Fourth of July. I gasp for air, my heart racing as my body quivers, and I spill my seed inside her.

Her legs fall away as I collapse on top of her, breathing heavily.

"Sweet Jesus," she whispers in my hair, swallowing and gasping right along with me.

Our bodies stick together, the fine sheen of perspiration acting as a binder. "I'm sorry."

"For what?" she asks as she touches my face.

"I wanted that to take longer."

She laughs softly. "Don't be silly. It was perfect." She lifts her head and kisses me, wiping away any doubt I might have had.

Rolling onto my side, I pull Tilly with me and wrap her in my arms.

"Angelo," she whispers and peers up at me.

"Yeah, baby?" I brush the hair away from her face.

"We didn't use protection." She grimaces.

"Fuck, I'm sorry. I got carried away."

"I forgot too. I haven't thought about condoms in…" Her voice drifts off.

"I'm clean," I tell her, trying to put her mind at ease.

"Pregnancy," she reminds me and runs her fingernails down the middle of my chest.

"It won't happen again. I promise."

There're no other words spoken, and the only sounds in the room are our harsh breaths and beating hearts.

I HAVEN'T MOVED in an hour. I've been staring at Tilly as she sleeps, feeling more content than I have in years. There's no overwhelming guilt or remorse for what happened last night—only happiness, which I haven't felt so completely in far too long.

The sunlight streams through the window above the bed, cascading across Tilly's naked body and making her look almost angelic. She turns a little as the sheet falls away, exposing her breast in all its perfection.

There isn't anything about her I don't like. She's as sweet as her cupcakes, caring, kind, and thoughtful. She loves the kids, and Tate has a soft spot for Tilly too. Marissa would've liked her if they'd met. They certainly would have become friends and probably stirred up a little trouble in the neighborhood.

Tilly's eyes open slowly. "Good morning." She stretches. "How long have you been awake?"

"Just a few minutes," I lie because I don't want to seem like a weirdo for watching her sleep for so long. "I didn't want to wake you."

She reaches out, placing her hand on my arm, and gazes at me from her pillow. "Did you sleep okay?"

"I haven't slept that well in years."

"Me either," she says, fighting to keep her eyes open.

I grab her hip and pull her body toward me as I scoot across the bed, closing the space between us. "Go back to sleep," I whisper as she relaxes in my arms and buries her face in my chest. "We're in no rush."

I could lie here all day with her body pressed up against mine, snuggling to keep the chill in the air at bay. There's nothing more perfect, besides making love to her, than holding her close and just being.

She peers up at me with her green eyes shining bright against her pale skin and auburn hair. "What time are the kids coming back?"

I brush the hair away from her face with the back of my fingers. "Not until later."

"I just wanted to make sure I didn't have to run out of here."

"There's no rush. Lucio isn't bringing them home until after dinner."

She molds her body against me, throwing her leg over mine. "Good. I could stay like this forever."

I hold her tight, inhaling the sweetness of her shampoo. "We don't have to move all day."

"Angelo."

I know what she's about to say is big.

"I never thought I'd feel this way again."

"Me either, Tilly."

"I'm happy for the first time in what feels like forever."

"I know. I almost forgot what it felt like to be at peace," I admit, knowing she'll understand exactly what I mean without taking offense.

No one else would fully grasp the depths of despair someone deals with after losing a spouse. The empty chair at dinner, the cold spot in the bed, and other things we all take for granted on a daily basis. It's not until the person is truly gone that we realize the finality of death and exactly what it means to be totally alone.

"Are we moving too quick?"

I touch her chin, making sure she's looking at me when I say the next words. "We waited years to find each other. We're two halves of the same soul. I think we were destined to meet. To suffer the same pain. To know each other's loss. We've rushed nothing."

"I feel like I've known you forever." She slides her hand up my arm, gripping my bicep. "People will think we're crazy."

"People can think what they want. How long did you date Mitchell before you fell in love with him?"

Marissa and I met in high school after her family moved to the old neighborhood from out of state. The moment I laid eyes on her, I knew I had to make her mine. There was no doubt in my mind that she was the girl for me. People thought I was nuts, but I loved her more than anything in the world.

"I don't remember a time when I didn't love him." She exhales softly.

I cup her face in my hands, wanting to kiss her so badly my chest aches. "We've been through more than most people twice our age. We know the preciousness of time and the fragility of life. There's no rhyme or reason when it comes to the heart."

Her hand glides down my arm and covers my hand. "I don't know what I did to deserve you, Angelo, but I'm thankful you came into my life."

"Baby, I've been asking myself that same question. We've got to stop thinking and just feel."

Leaning forward, I press my lips to hers. I'm done with words and questioning the speed we're moving. There's no controlling the pace at which it happens or containing the powerful punch to the gut when everything clicks.

Love is love, and there's nothing we can do to stop it.

CHAPTER TWENTY-ONE

TILLY

"YOU HAVE TO GET THAT," Daphne says as I stand in front of the dressing room mirror in the most decadent dress I've ever worn.

I glance down at the price tag and nearly have a heart attack. "It's six hundred dollars."

She bats my hand away from the tiny paper and grabs my hips, making me look at myself in the mirror. "Leo's paying," she says, like money is no object. "Your tits look incredible in this. Angelo will go bananas."

I stare at my reflection, loving the way the silk hugs my every curve, and she's right... My tits do look great. "I can't let Leo pay. That's not right. I'm not taking your money."

She moves closer and puts her mouth near my ear. "I have my own money." She stares at me intently in the mirror. "This is all him. Let the man pay. It makes him happy."

"It'll make him happy?" I blink quickly, confused.

She nods. "He wants us to have fun and relax. Money is no object to him. If you don't carry that dress out of this store, I'll just have it delivered to the bakery."

"Daphne, I really can't accept this."

"Oh my God. Look at you," Delilah says as she walks out of the dressing room, wearing leather pants and a sequined camisole which barely covers her belly. "Damn, girl."

They both gawk at me in the mirror as I twist my hands together in front of me.

"I know, right?" Daphne moves to my side and points to my chest. "Delilah, do you remember when your tits were this high?"

Delilah stalks toward us in a pair of black and gold leather boots. "Fuck. It's been years. Lulu killed my tits."

I laugh nervously as they both stare at my breasts like they've never seen anything more beautiful. It's awkward, but I know they're complimenting me.

"You'll see, Tilly." Daphne slaps my ass, and I yelp. "Angelo will have you preggers in no time."

My mouth falls open, and I freeze. "Um," I mumble as my face heats. "Let's not get ahead of ourselves."

"The Gallo men can almost just look at a woman and knock her up. You better be careful." Delilah laughs. "Look at me." She points toward her baby bump. "I never expected this to happen."

She has to be hands down the most adorable pregnant woman I've ever seen. With my luck, my ankles would swell up, making it impossible for me to wear heels.

"Jesus." Betty whistles as she walks into the dressing room area carrying no fewer than ten items draped over her arms. "Look at you ladies. Someone's getting lucky tonight."

"Ma, were any of us planned?" Daphne asks, crossing her arms and glancing in my direction.

"Oh, heavens no." Betty laughs. "I didn't want kids until I was thirty, but there was no stopping Santino."

"See." Daphne smirks, finally making her point loud and clear. "Told you."

Betty stands behind us and narrows her eyes. "What are you ladies talking about?"

"I told her to be careful because she could get knocked up."

Betty fumbles with the cross hanging around her neck. "Let's not scare Tilly away. Behave, girls."

"I'm not scared," I reply and straighten my back, standing taller than before. "I don't think we've gotten to that point yet. We're just finding our footing."

"So was I." Delilah laughs.

"Me too," Daphne adds.

"You'll be fine, dear." Betty touches my shoulder. "But if you wear that number around Angelo, all bets are off." She lifts an eyebrow. "It'll catch more than his eye."

"It's too expensive," I balk.

"Oh, please." Daphne shakes her head. "Leo won't even look at the bill."

I wonder what it's like to have so much money that six hundred dollars is like stopping at a coffee shop and ordering a latte. It's not something I can wrap my head around after scrounging up every last dollar I had to open the bakery.

"If it'll make you feel better, just get the one dress and nothing more," Delilah tells me as she bends down and runs her hand along her fancy boots.

"This would go great with my red heels."

"That would go great with anything, sweetheart." Betty walks into a dressing room and closes the door. "Get the dress."

"You heard her." Daphne pitches her head toward her mother's voice. "It's so you."

It's like they're twisting my arm to buy the dress, and even though I know it's a ridiculously expensive item, I want it. "Okay, but only if I can pay you back."

"Sure. You can pay Leo."

Delilah laughs. "That'll be fun to watch."

"If you're going to pay him back for that dress, you better at least get something else. He'll feel cheated," Betty calls out from the other side of the door.

"How about some sexy lingerie?" Delilah waggles her eyebrows as I step away from the mirror.

"Maybe." I run my fingers down the front of the dress, loving the smoothness against my skin.

"Something lacy." Daphne nods and steps back, looking me up and down. "Do you have a garter?"

"Of course." I laugh nervously. I so don't have a garter. Who wears garters in this day and age? Not a widow avoiding sex like the plague.

"We'll hook you up," Delilah says as she pulls at the waistband of her pants. "How can these be tight? They're freaking maternity pants, for shit's sake."

Daphne stares at Delilah's stomach and points to her tiny pooch. "Maybe you should lay off the cake."

"You better shut up," Delilah snaps and sucks in her gut until she practically turns blue. "Lucio keeps feeding me like I have a bottomless stomach."

I quietly excuse myself to change back into my real-world clothes, which aren't cheap, but are nowhere near as expensive as the dress Daphne's forcing me to buy.

"I'll meet you outside," I call out as I open the dressing room door, coming face-to-face with Daphne.

"We have lacy things to buy. We'll meet you two at the register."

"Works for me," Delilah says and grunts. "If I can ever get these damn things off."

"Leather's a bitch, kid," Betty tells her from the next stall.

Daphne grabs my hand. "Come on. We just need a few items."

An hour later and two full shopping bags in my hands, we finally walk out of the department store and climb in the car. I'm exhausted, not having spent that long shopping since I was in college.

"Who wants a drink?" Betty asks as she reapplies her lipstick while looking in the mirror hanging from the visor.

"Can we drink at the bar?" Daphne asks as she digs through her purse for something.

"I wish I could have a drink," Delilah grumbles.

"I could use more grandbabies," Betty says to Daphne. "You should try again soon."

"I wasn't trying with this one." Daphne ticks her head back toward me. "Look at her for another kid."

My head jerks back. "Me?"

"You're the new one," Delilah says.

My mouth hangs open. "We're taking things slow," I say, but I'm pretty sure everyone in the car knows what happened the other night.

"You keep telling yourself that," Daphne says, glancing at me in the rearview mirror.

"Tilly," Betty says, drawing my attention away from Daphne. "My son doesn't love easy, but he loves hard."

I bite my lip, trying to hide my smile.

"You can take things as slow as you want, but if you love him, don't wait an eternity to give me a baby."

I haven't thought about having children in so long.

After Mitchell died, I figured there was no hope. I'd be barren forever, living in perpetual widowhood and loneliness. But with the way these girls are talking, I'm going to be barefoot and pregnant in no time.

"I love this song," Daphne says, turning up the volume so loud none of us can talk.

I'm thankful for the noise, preferring not to talk about my sex life just yet. They have no problem sharing too much information with each other, but although they've made me feel welcome, I'm still an outsider.

It's a short trip back to the bar, and I excuse myself, needing a moment alone and wanting to drop off my bags at the bakery for later.

I send Roger a quick text, letting him know I survived the shopping spree, but just barely.

Roger: What's wrong?

Me: Nothing.

Roger: Tilly...

Me: Do you think we're moving too fast?

I tap my finger against the side of the phone and stand near the door, waiting for his reply. Roger's the one person who has kept me grounded and sane for the last five years. If shit's off, he'll set me straight.

Roger: Absolutely not. There's no timetable for shit like this. Just let yourself be happy.

Have I been denying myself all these years? That's what I get out of his text. Maybe I have, thinking somehow I'd be betraying Mitchell and the vows we said to each other. With Angelo, there's no fear or hesitation.

Me: Is he my rebound?

Roger: Stop questioning everything, Til. I don't like many people, but Angelo's solid. He's exactly who you need.

I read his message, feeling the exact same way. I don't know why I have doubts. Maybe I feel like I'm meant to be miserable, punished for some unknown cosmic reason. Why else would God take my husband? I think it's a question every person left behind asks themselves, but we never find the answer.

Me: I think I'm falling in love with him.

Roger: Then fall.

Those two simple words lift a huge weight off my shoulders. Roger's blessing means everything to me. No one has been there for me except him. He held my hand when I needed him. He wiped away my tears when I was inconsolable. He made sure I stayed alive when all I wanted to do was wither away and die.

I tuck my phone into my coat pocket and lock up the shop, ready to face Angelo and the ladies.

As I walk past the first set of windows, I search for the girls, but a couple embracing catches my eye.

I back up a few steps, shocked at what I see.

The hair on the back of my neck stands on end, and I feel my stomach sink.

Angelo's holding another woman in his arms. He's not just hugging her but embracing her. He whispers in her ear, and she smiles, wrapping her arms tighter around his body.

They're not strangers, that much is clear.

I stand outside the bar, staring through the window, unable to move. My world is crashing down for the second time in my life.

When he pulls his head back and kisses her cheek, lingering a little too long to be strangers, I gasp. But when she touches his face, staring into his eyes like she's loved him her entire life, I know I've been had.

"Fuck," I whisper, feeling like a fool.

I believed I was *the one*, but now there's nothing except darkness again.

CHAPTER TWENTY-TWO

ANGELO

MICHELLE GLANCES UP AT ME. "I'm so happy for you, Angelo." She wraps her arms tightly around my middle and sighs.

"Thanks, Michelle. I never thought I'd feel this way again."

I can see the sadness she tries to hide. "I knew we'd never work. I love you, though. Always have and always will."

"I love you too, Michelle." How could I not love her? She's been a part of my life since we were little kids. Although the spark was there, I didn't have the deep need to make her mine. It's unexplainable, but there was too much history between us to make it work.

"I met someone too," she says as she grips my side. "He's a big shot producer for a cable network."

"Does he treat you well?"

She nods. "So far."

"If he doesn't, I'll fly out to LA and kick his ass."

She smacks my arm. "Don't be silly. You know I can kick his ass all by myself." She laughs.

"That ain't no lie."

Daphne and Michelle could bring any man to his knees. Lucio and I made sure of it. We taught them how to fight dirty so they could defend themselves against any asshole on the streets. That was our duty as Daphne's brother, and since Michelle didn't have anyone at home to teach her those skills, we took her under our wing too.

"I better go. I want to talk to Daphne before I catch my plane. I'm only here until tomorrow to pick up some last-minute things I left behind."

I lean forward and kiss her cheek, saying goodbye to another person in my life. "Don't be a stranger, kid. You'll always be a part of our family."

"I hope you find some peace, Angelo," she whispers in my ear before kissing my cheek.

"I have," I tell her as I release her.

We walk toward the booth where my mother, Daphne, and Delilah are sitting, but there's no Tilly.

"Where's Tilly?"

They look at each other before turning their gazes on me.

"She said she'd be here in a minute, but that was a while ago." Ma shrugs. "I'm sure she'll be here soon."

Daphne pats the leather seat next to her and motions to Michelle. "Sit."

I peer out the windows, but the street is empty. My stomach knots because something's off. "I'm going to check on her."

"God, I hope we didn't scare her off," Delilah says as I start to walk away.

I back up, not liking how that sounded because I know exactly how these three ladies can be. I narrow my eyes on Ma. "What happened?"

Ma takes a slow sip of her beer, staring at me over the rim with wide eyes. I cross my arms and wait, because I need answers, and I'm not going anywhere until I get them.

"Nothing." She doesn't look me in the eyes.

I lift an eyebrow. "Nothing?"

"The girls just told her about the virility of the Gallo men."

"Fuck," I hiss, worrying she's been scared off by a day of shopping and Gallo gossip.

"Oh, come on." Daphne rolls her eyes. "She was laughing. We didn't traumatize her. She's probably busy with something. We did monopolize her time all day."

I glance toward the doorway again. "I'll be back. So help me God…"

"He's such a worrywart," Daphne says as I push through the front door and leave.

I pull on the door to the bakery, but it's locked and the lights are off. "Fuck," I groan as I peer up at the sky and close my eyes.

I storm back into the bar, ignoring my mother as she calls out to me and head into the office to grab my keys. There's no text from Tilly, but I send her one as I head toward the parking lot.

Me: Where are you?

I stare at my phone as I walk toward my car, hoping she'll reply, but she doesn't. The message doesn't even change to read. There's radio silence, and her car's missing.

"Angelo," Daphne calls out from the doorway as I climb into my car. "Where are you going?"

"She's gone." I slam my door, not needing to say anything else.

My hands are shaking as I turn the key in the ignition. I place my phone in my lap and pull out onto the street, heading toward her place. To add to my aggravation, traffic is a bitch, and there's an accident on Western Avenue.

A half hour later, I pull in front of her apartment building. Before I'm out of the car, Roger steps outside and closes the main door.

"Where is she?" I stalk toward the entrance.

Roger crosses his arms, and his nostrils flare. "She doesn't want to see you."

I narrow my gaze. "I don't understand."

Roger raises an eyebrow and doesn't move. "I should really kick your ass."

My head jerks back, because I'm confused as fuck. "For what?"

"You hurt her." He widens his stance, puffing out his chest.

My heart races as I drag my hand through my hair, still not understanding what's going on. "How?" I take a step forward, but he puts out his hand and blocks me.

He ticks his head toward the street. "Just go."

I throw out my arms, because there's no way in hell I'm leaving until I know exactly how I fucked up. "I'm not going anywhere. Not until you tell me what the hell is going on."

"You know what you did."

This guy is cryptic as fuck. I didn't do a goddamn thing. I worked all day, and then the girls came back. Nothing else happened.

"Man, come on. Help me out here. I'm totally at a loss. Just let me talk to Tilly."

He shakes his head. "I thought you were better than this. I never would've let you near her if I knew you were such an asshole and a player."

Player? I draw my eyebrows together. "I am not and have never been a player."

The only person I'm seeing and am completely in love with is Tilly. There's been no one else in my life.

Roger grunts.

"Tilly!" I move forward, and Roger hits me square

in the chest. I look down at where our bodies are touching, and I tighten my fists at my sides. "I'm being nice because you're her best friend, man, but let there be no doubt… You won't stop me from seeing her."

"Why don't you go bother the other woman you're seeing?"

I widen my eyes as I stagger backward. *The other woman?* Michelle. *Fuck.* My stomach drops, and my heart rate speeds up. I cover my heart, feeling like someone's sucker-punched me right in the gut.

"I'm not seeing anyone else, Roger. There's only Tilly. If you're talking about Michelle, she's a family friend and nothing more."

He sneers. "Tilly saw you kiss her."

My muscles tense. "On the fucking cheek, man. I've known her since I was in elementary school, and she's moving out of state." I close my eyes for a second and try to control my anger. "I was saying goodbye to her."

He shakes his head. "That's not how Tilly saw it."

I point toward the door, but I don't move. "Let me explain."

"No. I think it's best if you leave."

I peer down at the ground, knowing I can't just go. That's not how I'm wired, and I'm not going to let whatever Tilly thinks she saw fester until it's an unhealable wound.

"I'm not leaving."

"Then we have a problem," he says as his top lip curls.

"Roger." I stare him straight in the eyes. "I love Tilly."

"Hmm," he mutters, raising an eyebrow.

I push up my sleeves, determined to see her even if I have to spill my guts to a virtual stranger. There's no one more important in Tilly's life than Roger, and if he has to be the first one to hear the words, so be it.

"I mean it. I love her. Not just as a friend, but as so much more. I haven't felt this way about another person since Marissa died. I know it's crazy." I rub the back of my neck, wishing I were saying these words to Tilly and not her brother-in-law. "I know it's fast and probably doesn't make much sense to you. But Tilly and I were meant to be. We're fated. It's destiny. She's captured me completely. I freaking love her, Roger. I don't throw that word around without meaning it either. I love Tilly!" I yell the last words, hoping like hell she can hear me.

He turns and glances toward her apartment. "She can't hear you." He drags his hand down his face and groans. "What a fucking mess."

"Please," I beg. "I need to talk to her."

"Listen." He kicks at the ground, finally relaxing his posture. "She's fragile."

"I know," I whisper because I understand everything she feels so completely it's ridiculous.

"I've known Tilly for a decade, and the only other man she's ever been this crazy about was my brother." He shakes his head slowly and stares at me. "If I let you in, you have to promise me you're going to love her hard, be faithful forever, and always protect her."

"I swear. I'd never hurt her," I promise because I'd put any man who made Tilly cry in the ground.

You're that asshole right now, Angelo. I grimace, knowing how badly I fucked up.

"If you're playing her or lying to me, I will hunt you down."

I nod quickly. "I wouldn't expect anything less."

He stares off into the distance and sighs. "She's going to have my balls for this."

"She won't. I need to talk to her. I want her to know what she saw was nothing."

He rubs his neck and steps to the side. "Make shit right. Tell her how you feel. She needs to hear it."

I reach for the door handle and stop, turning to face Roger. "I will. I swear."

He juts his chin toward the building. "Go get her. She's in her bedroom."

I take the steps two at a time, holding my breath the entire way until I'm inside her apartment. Before I reach her bedroom door, I stop and peer into the room. Her body's draped across the bed, and she's crying.

My heart breaks as I push open the door.

"Roger?" she asks without turning around.

I step inside and close the door, ready to set shit right.

CHAPTER TWENTY-THREE

TILLY

I BURY my face in the crook of my arm and close my eyes. "Go away."

His footsteps are heavy on the hardwood floor, but I don't dare look up. He's gutted me enough for one day. What the hell was Roger thinking, letting Angelo upstairs? He promised me he'd make sure Angelo went away.

The bed dips next to me. "Tilly." Angelo's voice is soft and sweet, but I know better. "Look at me, baby."

"Don't 'baby' me." I bury my face deeper into the comforter, refusing to shed another tear. I'm too angry to be sad. I'd slap him across the face if I could look at him without bursting into tears.

"I know what you saw, but it's not what you think."

"I think you were touching someone who isn't just a friend." My voice is muffled by the blanket.

"That's Michelle. Daphne's best friend since elementary school. She worked at the bar up until a few weeks ago. She moved to California and just stopped in."

Stopped in and had her hands all over my man. Not just her hands, but her lips too. There's a difference between a hug you give to your friends and one you give to someone who's more intimate. "She's more than a friend, Angelo. I'm not blind. Did you sleep with her?"

"Never," he says quickly.

"Kiss her?"

"No."

"Touch her in a way I don't touch Roger?"

He pauses for the first time, making my point for me.

"She's more than a friend, then." I swallow down the lump in my throat and take a deep breath, trying to calm myself down.

"I never loved Michelle."

"What's that have to do with anything?"

Angelo's eyes always express so many emotions and I want to look at him, but I can't. I know I look like an idiot. I still have my head buried, and my eyes are puffy and swollen from crying. I'm the epitome of a hot mess.

"I made love to *you*. I said you're *mine*. Those aren't things I do with friends. I love *you*, Tilly."

The pain in my chest shifts and is replaced by a dull ache. "Say it again," I tell him, because hearing him say those words is everything to me.

"Sweetheart." He touches my back so softly, I almost don't feel his hand. "Look at me."

"I can't." I sniffle. "I'm a mess."

He slides his hand under my stomach and pulls me upright. I look down, because I know my face isn't pretty, but he touches my chin and forces my eyes to his.

"I love you, Tilly," he says again, gazing at me with the softest eyes.

My vision blurs again, and my stomach flips. "I love you too, Angelo," I whisper as my bottom lip trembles.

I never thought I'd say those words again. Never thought I'd feel this way again about anybody besides Mitchell. It's unexplainable and completely undeniable, mixed with a hint of crazy.

He slides his hand across my cheek, and my spine tingles. I melt into his touch as he cups my face. "There's no one else in this world for me except you. I'm sorry I hurt you. I'm sorry for causing you pain. I'm sorry for the tears on your beautiful face," he says as he wipes my cheek with his thumb. "I never want to cause you pain."

I blink through the tears, letting them fall. "I'm sorry I jumped to conclusions. I was just so hurt." I grab his hand that's resting on my knee. "I love you, Angelo."

His head dips forward, and I close my eyes, waiting for his lips to touch mine. "Promise you'll talk to me first before you run away."

I open my eyes and stare into his. "Are there more women in your past?"

"There's only you, and you're my future," he says before he kisses me, stealing every last bit of my breath and taking my entire heart too.

I climb into his lap as he wraps his arms around my body, holding me tight. There's something about the way he holds me that makes me feel more protected than I ever have before.

There's comfort in his touch and strength in his kiss, and it's completely intoxicating.

I reach down and palm his stiff cock. "I want you," I tell him.

His eyes widen. "Right now?"

I nod slowly and start rocking against his jeans, dry-humping him. "We can just do this too," I tell him, teasing the fuck out of him because I know I'm going to get my way.

He lifts me into the air, placing my feet on the floor, and stands in front of me. His fingers are at his zipper, and he motions to me with his head. "Undress," he tells me. "Now."

I push down my skirt, wanting to climb the man like a tree and mount him. I watch in awe and amazement as he pushes his pants to the floor and that beautiful cock of his makes its glorious appearance.

As soon as my clothes are off and he's naked enough to fuck, I use all my body weight to tackle him. "I'm not going to be gentle, and there's going to be nothing slow about this," I tell him as I slide my throbbing pussy against his cock.

"Condom," he whispers.

I put my finger over his lips, needing to feel his bare skin against mine again. "I'm clean," I say, feeding him the line he gave me last time.

In all the years I was with Mitchell, we never used birth control, and never once was my period late. The doctor said I'd need medical intervention to get pregnant, so fucking Angelo with no protection isn't an issue.

I rear up, lifting my lower half above him using my knees. He gazes up at me as he grips my hips, stopping me. "I'm yours, Tilly," he says before I slam my pussy down on his long, thick shaft.

He gasps, writhing underneath my weight as I buck, riding him hard and rough. I straighten my back and grind my clit against his hard flesh, driving myself closer to orgasm.

"Tell me again," I say as I lift myself up, waiting to hear the words.

His fingers dig into my hips, trying to make me move, but I'm not budging. "I'm yours," he repeats as he tightens his grip on me.

I ride him hard, fast, and unrelenting as I steady myself against his body, using my fingertips to balance against his ridiculously hard pecs. I gasp when he lifts his ass upward, meeting my thrust and driving his cock deeper.

"You're mine," he grunts, flipping the script as he pounds into me from underneath. His hands are still on my hips, controlling and directing my movements. "Always mine."

CHAPTER TWENTY-FOUR

ANGELO

TATE CRAWLS into my lap and curls her tiny body against my chest. "Daddy." She peers up at me with her big blue eyes. "Is Tilly going to be our new mom?"

There's no manual for these types of questions, but there sure as hell should be. There're a million manuals on feeding, sleeping, and ways to raise your kids without killing them in the process. But I haven't found anything that has taught me how to deal with the death of a parent and finding a new love that's worth a damn.

I kiss her hair and inhale the sweet strawberry scent of her baby shampoo. "Baby, your mom will always be your mom."

She blinks a few times as her lips purse. "I know, but what's Tilly going to be?"

I hold her tightly, wishing I could keep her this size forever. "What do you want her to be?"

I've learned a lot about life from my kids. They have an enduring ability to see the good in all things, no matter how dark shit gets. They view everything differently from adults, even relationships. Their minds aren't cluttered with hurt from the past, even though they've lost more than most at their young ages.

Tate pulls at her bottom lip as she stares at me. "Is she going to live with us?"

Tate's getting way ahead of herself, but I can't deny I've thought about what the future's going to hold. We haven't talked about if we're going to live together or get married. We're still too new for me to pull the trigger on something so big.

If it were just me, I'd have no issue jumping the gun and marrying Tilly, making sure she's mine forever. But with the kids…everything is hard. I have to think ten steps ahead and make sure I'm not going to fuck up their little minds.

"Not yet."

Her eyebrows furrow. "Why?"

"Tilly has her own place, baby."

"Can she sleep over sometimes?"

I laugh softly. "Do you want her to?"

Tate nods quickly. "She's fun."

"And I'm not?"

"Well." She glances away. "Sometimes you are."

I try not to let her words slay me, even though there's a bite to them. I know I haven't been the most fun parent the last few years. My head's been elsewhere, and my heart's been broken. Tilly's like a breath of fresh air carrying cupcakes and smiles, while I'm the grumpy bastard who doesn't always want to have a tea party.

"You're right." I look down at her. "She is fun."

"She and I can play dress-up and eat cupcakes."

There's the food. There's always food on her mind. I'd love for Tilly to be here, playing with the kids. They need a woman's touch and love. No matter how hard I try, I can't be all things at once. I've tried to be the mother and the father, but it's nearly impossible.

I don't think my kids are lacking in love. My parents and siblings shower them with so much affection, they never wonder if they're loved.

"Do you think we can have cupcakes for breakfast when Tilly sleeps over?"

"Cupcakes are dessert."

"Cupcakes can be anything we want," she tells me like she's the one in charge.

"We'll talk about it when she's here."

She nods. "I really like Tilly, Daddy. Grandma likes her too."

"Oh yeah?" I raise an eyebrow.

Tate's probably heard more than she should have hanging around with my mother—and especially from Daphne.

"Grandma said she's good for you."

Good isn't even the right word to describe everything Tilly is to me. She is better than good. She makes me want to be my best self. She's reminded me that I still have the ability to love. I thought I'd be alone for the rest of my life, never meeting anyone who understood my pain until Tilly came into my life.

"She is, Tate."

"She reminds me of Mommy. She's always happy," Tate tells me.

Marissa was never without a smile on her face. She would light up a room. All eyes would be on her, trying to soak up her goodness. Tate has the same gift, and every day I see so much of Marissa in her. It comforts me to know I have a piece of her with me always.

"I'm happy too."

Tate laughs. "No, you're not." She twists her hands in her lap and glances down. "You are now, but you haven't been."

I feel like a shit father, but I'm not the type of guy that can hide my feelings. I tried my best around the kids. Did everything I could to shelter them from my rage and hurt, but clearly, I wasn't as good at it as I thought I was.

I lift her chin, needing to see her cute little face. "I'm sorry, Tate."

There's been so much guilt since Marissa died. The sadness is always there, but the guilt sometimes can be suffocating. I know I could've done better. I should've been able to focus more on the kids and not on my sadness, but it took me a long time to get past the anger and hurt. Longer than I had expected or wanted.

"I love you, Daddy." She smiles.

There's nothing better than hearing those words.

"I love you too, baby."

She wiggles free of my hold and slides down my leg. "So, how about we play princesses?"

I growl softly. I'd rather stick needles in my fingertips than play princesses, but I can't break my kid's heart. She's playing me like a fiddle, knowing she has me right where she wants me.

"Sure," I say. Who can say no to that face? I thought it would be easier to put my foot down the older she got, but I've failed miserably.

She's my weak spot.

"Really?" Her mouth hangs open. "You can be Cinderella."

My head jerks back. "What if I want to be Belle?" I tease.

She touches her chest. "I'm Belle."

"Can I be the Beast, then?"

'Cause let's face it. I'm a shit princess.

"Can I play?" Brax asks as he walks into the living room, carrying his baby blanket and letting it drag on the hardwood floors behind him.

Tate turns around and stares at him for a second. "Fine," she says with a sigh. "You can be…" Her voice trails off.

I prepare myself for whatever crazy thing she's about to say that's probably going to make Brax cry. There's a tiny demon in her that gets joy out of terrorizing her brother.

"You can be the teacup."

His eyes light up. "Yay!"

The kid's weird, but he probably would've been happy if she'd made him a rug because at least she didn't tell him no and to get lost.

"You two have to do whatever I say." She glances from Brax to me with a serious face. "I'm the princess."

I'm already not liking the sound of this. Tate's bossy to begin with, and given free rein, she'll be a complete diva. "How about we just watch the movie instead?"

She twists her body and chews at her lip. "Only if I can make popcorn."

"Butter?" I ask like an idiot.

She looks at me like I have three heads. "Daddy, who likes popcorn without butter?"

"Get your pillow and blankets, and Brax and I will make the popcorn," I tell her because I'm not going to argue with the kid about butter.

She'd probably bathe in it if I let her.

She runs to her bedroom, leaving Brax and me alone. "You okay with watching the movie again, buddy?"

He nods slowly and lifts his blanket near his face. "It's scary sometimes."

"Come here," I tell him and motion for him to come to me.

He runs across the floor, almost tripping on the shredded blanket he refuses to give up. I don't have the heart to take it from him either. Not as long as it makes him happy, even if it's about to disintegrate.

"I'll protect you from the Beast, Brax. I love you," I tell him as I hug him tightly.

My kids can never hear those words enough from me. I say them daily, hoping that when they're older and I'm no longer here, they'll always remember they were loved. I'd do anything for them. I'd give my life if it meant they would be happy and healthy.

"I love you too, Daddy."

I ruffle his brown hair. "You want to help me make popcorn?"

"I want my own."

"We'll each have our own bowl."

The last thing I want is them fighting over the popcorn. Tonight's family night, and I could use a little peace and quiet. I don't want Tate flipping her shit because Brax is hogging the food, or God forbid, I do.

An hour later, after only one yelling match about who's going to sit on which side of the couch, the popcorn is gone and the kids are glued to the television. They're curled into my side as I hold them against me and close my eyes.

CHAPTER TWENTY-FIVE

TILLY

My hands shake as I unlock the front door to the shop. I barely slept, and after spending an unbelievable amount of hours prepping for today, I realized I need to hire help. I can't do it alone. I don't want to either. At least, not since Angelo's come into my life.

I never thought this day would get here.

When I finally decided to open a cupcake shop, I knew it would take time to find the perfect location, the right recipes, and make my dream a reality. But the process took longer than I expected and hit a few snags along the way.

Originally, I signed a lease a few blocks away, but

the building burned down after an electrical fire, pushing back my timeline. I was horrified, crying for days and feeling like I'd never find a new location. Everything I'd worked so hard for seemed out of reach.

"It's the big day," Roger says as he walks in behind me.

"You're not helping." I run my hand down the front of my skirt. Taking a deep breath, I turn to face him. "How do I look?"

"Like a sex kitten." He smirks. "Angelo will like it."

It's funny how things work out. I was devastated by the fire, but if that hadn't happened, I never would've met Angelo Gallo. So many things would be different, and my life and heart wouldn't be as full.

I grimace. "I wasn't going for the sex kitten look."

Roger snorts. "Then you should've worn Crocs and scrubs, because that outfit—" he points to me, swiping his finger up and down in the air "—doesn't scream anything except sex."

I flick my gaze upward. "Why do I keep you around?"

"Because life would be boring without me," he says as he stalks toward me. He grabs my shoulders, holding me at arm's length in front of him. "I need to be serious for a minute."

I nod and swallow down my nerves.

"I'm proud of you, Tilly. Mitchell would be proud of you too."

My nose tingles, and my vision blurs. "Don't make me cry."

He tightens his grip on my shoulders. "There's no time for tears, babe. You did something amazing here. Look around. This is all because of you."

I take it all in as he turns me around, remembering the day I got the keys. The place was an absolute mess. There wasn't a surface that didn't need to be replaced or painted. "What if it fails?"

Roger shakes his head. "It won't."

I wish I had his optimism, but I know the realities of a new business, especially in the crowded and sometimes saturated market of Chicago.

"Now take a deep breath and try to relax."

I laugh. Relax? Seriously, who can relax when they're opening a business they've sunk every dollar they have to their name into? There's no relaxation because if I can't fill the shop and sell out of cupcakes each day, I'll be penniless.

"This neighborhood needed a fun little shop like this. Plus, you have catering contracts already in place."

"I'm going to stay positive. I can do this." I nod.

Roger looks over my head toward the door. "Look who's here."

My eyes widen as I glance over my shoulder.

Roger releases my shoulders. "Looks like you have your first customers."

"We wanted to be your first." Betty walks into the shop, followed by the entire family.

"I can't believe you all came," I say quickly, barely able to stand still.

Tate's the first one to reach me. "I love your cupcakes." She peers up at me, buttering me up, and I'd be lying if I said it wasn't working.

God, I don't know how her father ever tells her no. Her face is so beautiful, and her smile is like her father's.

"Can I have one?" she asks as I touch the pink bow in her hair.

"Of course." I bend down, coming eye-to-eye with the little Italian princess. "What flavor?"

Angelo places his hand on Tate's shoulder and stands behind her. "Tate, why don't you go see what you want and let me talk to Tilly for a second."

I gaze upward at his handsome face. Six months ago, I was lonely, starting a business to fill my days so I wouldn't have to think about the emptiness. Now, my world is filled with this big, crazy Italian family and a man who has reminded me what it feels like to be loved.

"Come on, sweetheart. Let's pick out something good." Betty takes Tate's hand and leads her away, giving us some privacy.

"Can I have more than one?" Tate asks her grandmother.

I laugh as I stand, coming face-to-face with the man who's swept me off my feet. "Hi," I say softly.

He moves closer and kisses me. "Hey, yourself." He

stares at me with those beautiful blue eyes. "What time does the shop close?"

"Seven."

"We're going to celebrate. I'll bring the champagne." He stares into my eyes.

"I'll bring the frosting." I waggle my eyebrows, and he smirks.

Lucio clears his throat. "That's about enough of that. There are kids present."

I laugh as Angelo smacks Lucio's chest with the back of his hand. "Don't be a downer."

"This place is amazing." Daphne stands in the middle of the bakery with her mouth hanging open. "It's like every little girl's dream."

I giggle and tick my head toward Tate. "She enjoys it."

Daphne rolls her eyes. "That girl is a bottomless pit."

"She's adorable."

"She wants you to sleep over," Angelo says, catching me completely off guard.

My eyes widen. "She does?"

"She does. She also wants cupcakes for breakfast." He wraps his arm around my waist as he comes to stand next to me. "I think I would be okay with that if you were there."

"You're great and all, but I think she misses having a girl around." I nudge my hip into him. "For all those tea parties and princess costumes."

"I clearly lack in the princess department."

I rest my head on his shoulder and watch as his family gawks at the cupcake display. "Thanks for coming today. It means a lot. I can't believe everyone came," I tell Angelo.

"Baby, the Gallos do everything in groups."

"I'm finally understanding that."

When my parents died, I didn't think I'd ever be a part of a close-knit family again. Mitchell's parents live in the Caribbean, preferring the sunshine and turquoise waters to the chill of Chicago. I have Roger and I love him like my own brother, but holidays are never anything crazy with only a handful of people. But the Gallos... They're like something right out of a fairy tale.

ANGELO WALKS into the kitchen area just after seven and freezes. He lifts an eyebrow and smirks when he sees me wearing nothing but my heels and an apron.

I wave my hand in front of the small buffet of every cupcake topping I had on hand and three different colors of frosting. "Put the champagne down and take off your pants."

His eyes burn bright as he unzips his pants and pushes them down his legs, never taking his eyes off me. I grab his hand and pull him toward the table. "Sit or stand, but I have a feeling you may get weak in the knees." I smirk because I'm going to deliver so much pleasure with my mouth, he's going to have a hard time staying upright.

Angelo hops up on the table, jumping a little when the cold steel touches his ass. "Fuck," he groans.

I fist his cock, making him forget about the cold bite of the table. "This is going to get messy."

His eyes light up. "I've never been afraid to get dirty."

I lick my lips, and his cock twitches against my palm. He reaches out, and I shake my head. "Hands to yourself, big boy."

He grunts as I reach for the first bowl of frosting and grab a giant glob with two fingers. "I have to taste test some new combinations, but a girl can only eat so much cake."

His eyes widen. "How many?"

"Five," I say as I cover the tip of his penis with raspberry frosting.

He groans as I stick my fingers in my mouth, sucking the last bits of frosting from the tips. I'm doing it slowly, knowing it's sweet torture as he follows my mouth with his eyes.

I grab a bowl of white chocolate shavings and move it closer. "I'm going to enjoy this."

As the last bit of chocolate adorns the frosting, I lean forward, dragging my tongue over the tip. Not enough for it to penetrate the gooey goodness, but just enough to have the man on edge and breathing shallow.

His fingers curl around the side of the table as he tries to steady himself. "Jesus, Tilly." His voice wavers. "You're trying to kill me."

"Hmmm." I take another lick. "There's something missing."

"Maybe my cock in your mouth," he says as I straighten, leaving his dick twitching.

"Tsk. Tsk. Don't rush a master."

I grab the bottle of lemon syrup and drizzle it over the top of his dick, letting the gooey concoction drip down the sides. I lick my lips and want nothing more than to take him into my mouth. "That might work."

He stays silent, but he's begging me with his eyes. He lets out a shaky breath as I place my hands flat on the table next to his legs, hovering my open mouth over his sweet cock.

"So fucking good," he says as I use the tip of my tongue, swiping away the first layer of frosting. When his fingers tangle in my hair, I close my lips around the head and suck him upward instead of moving down. His ass rises off the table, and he drags in a breath, tightening his grip on my hair. "Fuck."

I love him with my mouth, sucking every last drop of frosting and sweetness from his skin. He's shaking, close to the edge and ready to explode, but I'm not ready for my taste test to end.

He gasps as my mouth slides off his cock. "Don't stop," he begs.

I shake my head. "We have four more flavors."

He groans and falls backward, lying flat on the table with his legs dangling over the edge. "Have your way with me," he says, and I'm more than happy to oblige.

I barely make it through the triple chocolate cherry surprise I've licked off his penis when he sits straight up.

"Enough," he says, hopping off the table and grabbing my waist. He turns me quickly, pinning me against the table. "I need to be inside you." He pushes down on the middle of my back, forcing my chest against the cold metal.

His cock is pressed against my pussy as he wraps my hair around his hand. "You're quite the tease, baby."

I shiver in anticipation. I look over my shoulder and smirk. "Teach me a lesson, big boy."

I barely get the words out before he thrusts into me, silencing my sarcasm. The edge of the table bites into my hips as he rocks into me, deeper and harder with each stroke.

I push back, meeting him blow for blow as our bodies slap together in complete harmony. This is how it's supposed to be. Primal, sexy, and filled with so much pleasure, I can barely stay upright.

His hand comes around my front, pushing between my legs and cupping my pussy. "This is mine," he says, and who am I to argue. He owns me completely.

When his fingers tweak my clit, I spiral over the edge as my body shakes uncontrollably and the orgasm pulls me under, almost causing me to black out.

He collapses over my back, gasping for air from the orgasm that no doubt just ripped through his body too. "Pure fucking heaven," he whispers against my skin.

That's exactly what it feels like every time I'm with Angelo. There's nothing sweeter.

CHAPTER TWENTY-SIX

ANGELO

"IT'S VEGAS, BABY." Vinnie moves forward in his chair, unable to sit still. "I never thought this day would come."

It's football draft day, something I've watched on television every year since I was a kid. Never in a million years did I think I'd be here waiting to hear my little brother's name being called to play pro ball.

Tilly wraps her hand around my bicep. "There're so many people here."

I glance around the large room at the thousand or more people packed inside like sardines, and I pull Tilly closer to my side. "This is the craziest thing I've ever seen."

"Vegas is a different world." She shakes her head.

"So is football," I tell her.

There's nothing like draft day, and with it being in Vegas this year, it's bigger and crazier than ever.

"God, please let Chicago call my name." Vinnie rubs his hands together and closes his eyes. "Please."

"It would be nice to have you home, kid," Daphne tells him as she strokes his arm, trying to calm him.

"Will you still love me if Green Bay drafts me?"

Lucio gags. "It'll be hard. Honestly, bro, I can't wear the green and gold even if it has our name on the back."

"I thought Chicago had that crazy chick you were trying to avoid," I say.

"She's the team owner's daughter."

"I thought you said she was hot?" Lucio looks confused, but he wasn't there when Vinnie told us what really happened.

Somehow, the chick got into Vinnie's dorm room and was waiting for him one night. Completely naked. She basically threw herself at him, professing her love, and saying they were meant to be together. Thankfully, and surprisingly, Vinnie called campus security instead of banging the chick. Which is surprising because, let's face it, Vinnie has never been one to say no to pussy.

But security didn't stop her from showing up on campus again, nor did his repeated attempts to explain that he wanted nothing to do with her. The chick was relentless and seemed to have eyes only for Vinnie.

Vinnie rubs his forehead and grimaces. "If hot means crazy as fuck, then yeah."

"You do attract a different breed," I tell him, trying to bite back my laughter.

"You'll never believe who we just saw," Pop says as he pulls out the chair next to Vinnie for my mother.

"Who?" Leo looks up from his phone, finally joining the conversation.

"Ditka." Pop's beams. "I never thought I'd see him again after what happened."

I raise an eyebrow. "What happened?"

"You don't want to know." Pop slides into the chair next to my ma and takes a sip of his beer, avoiding looking me in the eye.

With my father's past business dealings, anything is possible. The man knows half the city in one way or another. He's never been completely open about shit, but I'm happy I don't know everything. Some things aren't meant to be public knowledge or even shared among family.

"I'm so proud of you, sweetheart." Ma touches Vinnie's cheek.

"Ma, there's cameras." He moves his head to the side and away from her hand. "Not here. You're killin' my cred."

She narrows her eyes as she holds her hand in the air. "I don't care about your cred. I'll kiss your face if I want to."

Vinnie grunts as the camera that was at the next table turns toward him.

"Next up is Chicago," the announcer says into the microphone as the head of the football league walks out onto the stage.

"With the tenth pick in the first round, Chicago selects…"

Although some people in the room are on their feet chanting *Chicago,* you could hear a pin drop at our table. It's the only time I can remember the Gallos ever being completely silent.

"Vinnie Gallo, Quarterback from…"

It's impossible to hear the rest of his statement because the Chicago fans, along with my family, are on their feet, screaming at the top of their lungs.

As Vinnie stands, Ma grabs his face and plants a giant kiss on his cheek for the entire world to see. He doesn't fight her on it, rolling with it because he loves his mother and he doesn't want to look like a complete asshole to the millions of people who are watching.

When she finally releases him, he jogs up to the stage to meet the team's general manager and don the team hat for photos.

"Unbelievable," I mutter.

The kid did it.

Not only is he going to play ball for the home team, but he was picked in the first round, which means he's the best of the best. I'm almost teary-eyed watching my kid brother on the stage.

Tilly tucks herself into my side, screaming louder than I've ever heard her scream before. "Go Vinnie!"

I peer down at my girl.

"Fuck yeah!" Daphne screams, but it's barely audible beyond our table. We get a few looks, but whatever. They can go fuck themselves.

The moment is monumental but short-lived as the clock starts ticking down for the next draft pick.

"He did it." Ma claps. "My baby's coming home."

My father wraps his arm around her back. "He is, sweetheart. Big things are coming for him."

If by big things, he means tons of money, fame, a crazy-as-fuck chick, and probably a head ten times bigger than he already has…then, yeah.

"We have to celebrate," I say, knowing this is Vegas, and the city never sleeps.

I'm taking full advantage of a child-free weekend, and so is everybody else around the table. It's rare that we all have this kind of freedom, but Aunt Fran insisted she and Bear could handle watching the kids for a few days.

"Oh shit," Daphne says, pointing toward the stage and the team owner's daughter, who's waiting for Vinnie near the stairs.

"Fuck," I groan, knowing she's all kinds of trouble. The last thing Vinnie needs is a girl who's nuttier than a PayDay candy bar chasing after his ass off the field and distracting him when he's just starting his career.

Tilly tightens her hold on my arm, following my eyes. "She doesn't look so bad."

"She's the worst kind of trouble."

"I'm starving." Pop rubs his stomach and looks at my mother, who's not even paying attention to him. "Let's start with dinner, and we'll see what kind of trouble we can get into. I have a friend…"

"Oh, no." Lucio shakes his head and holds up his hands. "We're not going to some mafia joint. We're steering clear of your old *buddies*."

Vegas, which was started by mobsters, is no cleaner than it was fifty years ago. They've just learned how to hide in plain sight better, flying under the radar of the public and the authorities. My father seems to know people everywhere we go in this city, and it's not because of his charm or good looks.

"You pick the place, then," Pop tells Lucio.

"Angelo and I already made dinner reservations for the family, and we'll figure out the rest as we go. This is Vegas, and I'm not planning a night of drunken decadence." Lucio glances at Delilah. "I want to enjoy my woman a little bit."

Delilah flings her arms around Lucio and whispers something in his ear. By the look on his face, I'd say it was scandalous and exactly how I plan to finish off my night too. Minus Delilah and Lucio, of course.

"Vinnie said he'll meet us at the restaurant," Ma says as she glances at her cell phone. "Let's go. Nothing else can outdo that moment."

I have to agree. No draft before or after this one will ever come close to the feelings of pride and joy I experienced hearing my little brother's name being called.

Daphne stands, placing her purse under her arm. "Let's do this. I have liquor to consume."

"I feel a hangover coming on," Tilly says as she slides her hand into mine, standing from the table. "Don't let me get too drunk."

"I got you, baby," I say against her lips. "Always."

THE ENTIRE TABLE is staring at the menu in silence as we sit in the swanky steakhouse at our hotel. We're stalling and sipping champagne as we wait for Vinnie to finish up with the press. The day has already been monumental, and there's one more thing that needs to happen to make it perfect.

Something I've been planning on doing for weeks but haven't found the balls or the moment to pull the trigger. This isn't the most romantic location, but I don't think Tilly will care.

I lift my ass and kick the chair backward, dropping down on one knee. Tilly's eyes widen. She knows what's coming. I fish the ring out of my pocket after carrying it with me every day for just the right moment.

"Tilly, will you do me the honor of becoming my wife?"

Tilly gasps as tears fill her eyes.

239

"Shut up." Daphne peers over Tilly's shoulder to get a look at the ring. "Say yes," she begs her.

Tilly covers her mouth with her hand and stares at me as tears stream down her face. "Yes," she whispers so quietly, I barely hear her.

I grab her hand away from her face and slip the two-carat princess-cut ring onto her finger. "I love you, Tilly."

She falls forward into my lap, almost knocking me over. "I love you, Angelo. Yes. Yes. I want to be your wife."

EPILOGUE

TILLY

I STEP in front of the full-length mirror and blink a few times. I never thought I'd be here again, wearing a dress made of decadent lace and the smoothest silk.

The door opens, and there's a small gasp. "You're so pretty," Tate says as she stands in the doorway at her grandmother's side.

She looks like such a little princess in her light pink lace dress, which matches mine exactly, and her crystal tiara I bought for her to wear today. This day is just as much about her and Brax as it is about Angelo and me. Their world is going to change forever, as will mine.

I turn, motioning for her. "Come here, sweetheart."

She runs toward me and wraps her tiny arms around

my body, smashing her face into my dress. "I'm so happy," she says.

"Can you give us a minute?" I ask Betty, wanting to talk to Tate before the wedding.

"Sure, dear." Betty gives me a quick nod before closing the door, leaving us alone.

I take Tate's hand and guide her toward the couch. She practically jumps into my lap, not caring that we're all dressed up, ready to walk down the aisle. She swipes her long brown hair away from her face and stares up at me with her big blue eyes.

"Are you ready?" I ask her.

She nods. "I'm so happy," she whispers, somehow containing her excitement, but she's shaking.

"How's your daddy?"

"He looks so handsome."

Angelo looks handsome in everything he wears. The man wears pajama pants like nobody's business, and when he's shirtless…don't even get me started.

"Is he okay?"

She nods quickly. "He's excited."

"Are you happy?" I ask, because nothing is more important to me than this little girl's happiness.

She turns in my lap and places her hand on the exposed skin above my sweetheart neckline. "I am."

"Good." I squeeze her tightly, kissing her plump cheeks, careful not to smudge my lipstick or leave any behind.

Her fingers find my diamond pendant. "Brax and I have a question," she says, sounding so grown-up.

"Anything, baby."

She glances down for a second and shifts. "We want to know if we can call you Mom."

My vision blurs. Never in a million years did I think this kid was going to ask me that question just before I walked down the aisle. My heart races, and my chest is so full of joy and love, I'm not sure my body can take much more.

"Would you like that?" I can barely get the words out without bursting into tears.

Tate nods. "We need a mommy."

"You have one, sweetheart." I brush her hair off her shoulder. "She may not be here with you, but she'll always be yours."

"Cole has two mommies."

"Yes, he does," I tell her, but I don't say anything more. I reach out and cup her face in my hands. "I'd be the luckiest woman in the world to have you as a daughter, Tate. Nothing would make me happier."

Her little body vibrates with excitement. "This is the best day ever."

"It's almost time," Roger says from the doorway, looking stunning as always in his pristine and over-priced suit. "Are you ready?"

"One second," I tell him before returning my full attention to Tate. I wrap my arms around her, hugging her tightly. "I love you, Tate."

"I love you too, Mommy," she says before wiggling out of my arms and dashing to the door right past Roger.

The tears I've somehow held in start to fall, growing in intensity as the power and importance of her last words hit me.

"Oh shit. Don't cry. You're going to mess up your makeup." Roger stalks toward me, pulling a tissue from the box sitting on the table near the doorway.

"Did you hear her?" My words come out garbled because my face is scrunched up in the worst ugly-cry expression ever. It's not pretty, and I'm glad she waited to say those words until we were alone.

Roger nods. "Kid's got timing." He laughs as he bends down and hands me the tissue.

I press the soft cotton to my face, careful not to smear my makeup, which I'm sure is already running down my face. Roger reaches into his jacket and fishes out two envelopes.

"I have two letters for you today."

My eyebrows rise, and I know the floodgates are about to break wide open.

"One from your past and one from your future," he says as he places them in my hand. "Take your time reading them. The people will wait."

"Look at me," I say through my tears, noticing the mascara all over the tissue.

"I'll get Martin back here. He's the best drag makeup artist in Chicago. He can fix your face."

I laugh and cry at the same time, tightening my hold

on the envelopes.

"Breathe, Tilly."

I inhale, trying to calm myself down, even though there's no use. Whatever's inside these envelopes will undoubtedly do nothing to make the tears stop falling.

"I'll be back in a few minutes." Roger pats my hands before walking toward the door.

I stare up at him and take another deep breath. When he leaves, I glance down at both men's handwriting, trying to prepare myself for the emotional ass-kicking I'm about to receive.

I place Angelo's letter in my lap before carefully opening the envelope from Mitchell.

Tilly,

This isn't a goodbye. A love like ours will never have an end, existing like the greatest galaxies in the universe, but on different paths.

Today's your wedding day. Something I thought about when I made arrangements in case something unexpected happened to me. I knew you'd grieve my absence, close yourself off from the world, but I hoped Roger would help keep you going, reminding you of all the reasons life is so wonderful.

If you're reading this letter, you've found love again. I no longer have to worry about you being alone. I can finally rest, knowing you've found someone to love you like you deserve to be loved.

Just know I'm happy. Today should be filled with celebration and not sorrow. Stop mourning what you lost and look forward to all you've gained.

We're lucky to have one great love in our lifetime. I was blessed the day I found you. But you've found something rare again. Hold on to that. Cherish it. Give your all and remember the preciousness of each moment.

I'll be with you today and always. You may not see me or feel me by your side, but I'll watch over you until the day you take your last breath.

As you take the first steps down the aisle, look to the future and not the past. Let go of the hurt, bury the sadness and grief deep, and move forward to your future.

Live life well.

Be fierce.

Love strong and deeply.

And know I'll always love you.

Yours Always,

Mitchell

"I love you, Mitchell," I whisper as I fold the paper carefully. "Always."

Moments of our time together flash through my mind, playing like a sped-up movie reel. So much love. So much happiness. Then the grief of knowing I'd lost him forever.

I lift Angelo's envelope and close my eyes as I tear open the paper.

Tilly,

As you walk down the aisle today, know I'm only

looking forward to our future. Although our dark pasts have brought us together, forging a love and understanding no other two people can fathom, our souls will be joined eternally in love and happiness.

Our pasts define us. We cannot wipe away what happened or forget about what we've lost. Mitchell and Marissa will always be a part of who we are and the guiding force that has brought us together.

Today, I take you as my wife, making you mine forever and giving myself to you completely. Not only am I giving you my soul, but my family too. Tate and Brax are completely in love with you, and I know you'll love them as if they were your own.

I will always protect you from anyone who wishes you harm, and shelter you as best I can from any pain until I take my last breath.

Thank you for coming into my life and opening your heart, showing me that love is possible again. I thought my heart died that day, but you've brought me back to life and made me whole again.

Now, come to me, my love. We have a future to live.

I love you, Tilly.

Yours,

Angelo

Vinnie's coming! Vinnie's coming!

OMG!

Vinnie. Is. Coming!

It's about to get **wild** and **sexy** for this hot, new
professional football player!
… and he's about to be brought to his knees.

Visit ***menofinked.com/hustle*** to grab Vinnie!

MEN OF INKED: SOUTHSIDE SERIES
Maneuver - Book 1
Flow - Book 2
Hook - Book 3
Hustle - Book 4

please visit menofinked.com for information.

The Original Men of Inked

Visit **menofinked.com/free** to download your
FREE copy!

Sign up for my VIP newsletter, featuring exclusive
eBooks, special deals, and giveaways!
Visit menofinked.com/news-bm

Or

text **GALLOS** to **24587**
to sign up for VIP text news

Want to be the first to know about upcoming sales and
new releases? Follow me on BookBub too!

I'd love to hear from you.

Connect with me at:

www.chellebliss.com
Twitter | Facebook | Instagram
Join my PRIVATE Facebook Reader Group

Want a **TEXT MESSAGE** when I have a new release?
Text **GALLOS** to **24587**
(US & Canada Only... Sorry!)

Don't forget to download these **FREE** ebooks!

The Original Men of Inked

menofinked.com/free

ALFA Investigations Series

ABOUT THE AUTHOR

Chelle Bliss is the *Wall Street Journal* and *USA Today* bestselling author of Men of Inked: Southside Series, Misadventures of a City Girl, the Men of Inked, and ALFA Investigations series.

She hails from the Midwest, but currently lives near the beach even though she hates sand. She's a full-time writer, time-waster extraordinaire, social media addict, coffee fiend, and ex high school history teacher.

She loves spending time with her two cats, alpha boyfriend, and chatting with readers. To learn more about Chelle, please visit chellebliss.com.

JOIN MY NEWSLETTER

FOLLOW ME ON BOOKBUB

Text Notifications (US only)
➔ Text **ALPHAS** to **24587**

WHERE TO FOLLOW CHELLE:

WEBSITE | TWITTER | FACEBOOK |
INSTAGRAM
JOIN MY PRIVATE FACEBOOK GROUP

Want to drop me a line?

authorchellebliss@gmail.com
www.chellebliss.com

TAP HERE to sign up for my VIP newsletter, featuring exclusive eBooks, special deals, and giveaways!

Or

text GALLOS to 24587

to sign up for VIP text news

MEN OF INKED: SOUTHSIDE SERIES

Maneuver - Book 1

Flow - Book 2

Hook - Book 3

Hustle - Book 4

MEN OF INKED SERIES

Throttle Me - Book 1

Hook Me - Book 2

Resist Me - Book 3

Uncover Me - Book 4

Without Me - Book 5

Honor Me - Book 6

Worship Me - Book 7

Men of Inked Bonus Novellas

The Gallos

Resisting

Rebound (Flash aka Sam)

ALFA INVESTIGATIONS SERIES

Sinful Intent - Book 1

Unlawful Desire - Book 2

Wicked Impulse - Book 3

ALFA Investigations Novellas

Rebound (Flash aka Sam)

Top Bottom Switch (Ret)

NAILED DOWN SERIES

Nailed Down - Book 1

Tied Down - Book 2

TAKEOVER DUET

Acquisition - Book 1

Merger - Book 2

FILTHY SERIES

Dirty Work

Dirty Secret

Dirty Defiance

SINGLE READS

Mend

Enshrine

Misadventures of a City Girl

Misadventures with a Speed Demon

LOVE AT LAST SERIES

Untangle Me - Book 1

Kayden the Past - Book 2